To my incredible family
(Ross, Logan, Dad, and Mom),
You generous and loving friends, and
this great and unpredictable world...

THE YEAR OF CARTER HIGGINS

Prologue

From how I see things, our place on this Earth is absolutely temporary. No one is meant to live forever. We're all here just for a little while, just to see what this life is all about. Some may be here longer than others, but that only means they need more time to understand who they really are. And some are barely able to get a taste of life before they are forced to leave it because they already have all the answers they need.

At least, that's what I've learned from my experience living in Alliance, North Carolina; A nostalgic old place full of retired sailors and ex-cons, I can't picture a more fitting place to be temporary in.

Alliance has a feeling about it like it's trying to keep you there, as if you both can somehow mutually benefit from that kind of loose connection each time you say, *I live here*. As if one day it's expecting you to become one of those pale-eyed sailors or suspicious ex-cons. With its cool air brought in from the small and depopulated port we pretend we're proud of, the long narrow roads that seem to go on forever with more bumps etched in its asphalt than a small boy learning to ride a bike, the drug addicts that grin at me from the curb outside the new Exxon gas station. All those temporary things and more.

It's in this nurturing environment where I've grown up, created myself, and made some striking memories; the only things I know for sure to be absolutely real. Chasing ladybugs in my backyard, making snow angels in the gravel and dirt, feeling overall cheated by its lack of decent restaurants. My parents moved here solely because of the low real estate prices. It's a real wonder why.

It was winter when we moved into our little haven on 42 Fairview Circle. The winter my cat died because we didn't see her outside in the snow. A real moment of foreshadowing to get the hell out, or maybe some sort of welcoming gift from the town. Alliance has a dark sense of humour.

Our little suburban house is the most neutral shade of beige you can imagine with four windows in the front and four in the back. Symmetry is everything to my father. The yard is patchy and browning slightly with light spots of sun-scorched earth peeking out from beneath the green grass. To really show the world just how unadventurous we are, nearly every other house is some shade of jungle green or bright ocean blue. Thank God we're all too middle class to afford a HOA.

Now you may know this town or someplace like it, but you don't know me.

When it comes to it, I've always had a different perspective of the world than most people my age. Everything else may matter later, but we'll worry about that when it's relevant. Until then, you can fill in the blanks.

Now I'm sure it's easy to not care about me or my house or where I live or any of that stuff that, at the end of the day, doesn't really matter. So why read this? Why care? That reason spawns from how all things come to be. From one brief second of complete and unimaginable pain.

Everything has been redundant in my short seventeen years of life, for the most part. I knew that even as a seven-year-old girl living in a blue sweater with a mind full of nothing.

One of the days that I actually remember clearly from my childhood was one sunny day in the month of April, a day a bit more out of sync than the rest. The sky so full of light, fresh and moving, so fine you could see those little dust fairies floating in it. The air was crisp and refreshed from the removal of that bitter Winter, the end of the frost still settling in my cheeks and young bones.

My mom forced me to a 'welcome spring' block party we were having down the street. No one has those unless they're stupid by the way. I wore something bland and forgetful and tried to stand near the back of the party by the witch hazel bushes. I was a shy yet pretentious young girl even back then. I liked being by myself. I had a school friend or two but seeing them outside of the confines of a classroom was too personal.

My mom pointed at me as she was talking to a woman I didn't know from across the foldable picnic tables. Her face read something like, that's mine over there, unfortunately, the reason I get blackout drunk at block parties. Oh Martha.

I made eye contact for a short second then quickly swivelled my head in the other direction towards the bush next to me, my brown hair hitting me softly against my face. She waved me over with her hand but I shook my head. She narrowed her eyes and I shrunk deeper into the witch hazel bush. Rolling her eyes, and pointed again out towards the road. My brother Sam was playing basketball with his new friends in the street. I watched as he passed the ball and took a few shots.

I began to feel content for a moment, with no clear reason why, as the long and pale arm of my mother reached out from across her thin body. It's as if I had finally realized that things were good. Standing in the grassy area by my house surrounded by people who didn't know me and didn't really care. I felt so mundane and untouched. So shamelessly thankful for an otherwise thankless town. I know it's vague but I can't think of any other way to describe it. I do relish that feeling more than ever though.

I didn't know, at the young age of seven, what that feeling meant. I do now. I started feeling like that the moment I met Carter Higgins.

My mom approached me with the mystery woman in tow, both smiling a bit too widely at the little shy girl who just wanted to stare at a bush. Behind the woman stood a little boy in a shirt that was too big and a hat that was too small. He stood next to her with a soft half-smile on his face, swinging his arms slightly by his side.

"Honey, this is Mrs. Higgins. She lives just down the street. She's new like us."

I smiled awkwardly and pretended to be really interested in the bush.

Mrs. Higgins crouched slightly and brought the little boy forward.

"Hi, Dylan. How are you?"

"I'm fine."

"Well good. You have a very pretty name."

I smiled at a small space between her and the boy. People never really said that to me much. I guess no one was really impressed by a girl with a boy's name back then.

Mrs. Higgins whispered something to the boy and he stepped forward reluctantly.

"Hi."

I lifted my head again, eyeing my mom with contained anger, and stole a quick glance at his face. He was a freckled face boy with dark black hair and cute dimples. I instantly lost interest in the bush and felt my cheeks redden. They were always doing that.

"Hi."

"Say your name sweetie," Mrs. Higgins encouraged the boy.

"I'm Carter."

That's when I got that feeling. That warm and funny feeling I had in my stomach.

"I'm Dylan."

"Cool."

We stared at each other and the moms laughed. I focused on his face and felt my cheeks get a little redder.

Ten years later and that feeling still sleeps down in my stomach, keeping me warm sometimes throughout the year.

What people fail to tell you when you're seven is that feeling is really hard to come by. When you lose it, it's hard to find it again. And when I lost it 10 years later, it consumed me, blue sweater and all. Hatred and confusion blinded me from the light beyond my bedroom window. My own world of resentment was created towards everything and everyone. Alliance had lived up to its expectations of disappointment.

It's different seeing from that new perspective of reality. Seeing people smile, hearing the laughs, the crying, the everything; but never really having any of it yourself. I see the parts of life that others only get to live and look back on, wishing they'd have known it was the good old days.

They figure it out twenty years later, but I know now. It's a surreal feeling, like seeing yourself sleeping in a dream. Watching people be happy, it makes life a little easier to live in.
It's a promise for a day like that for myself.

Anyway, where am I now? After everything happened in secession. After I learned that I prefer to listen. I can't say exactly. But I hope that I can one day move on from this pain. I know this is not a traditional college admissions essay. But meeting Carter Higgins truly was the defining moment of my young life.

1.

Before

An old 2001 sand colored Camry with duct tape on the driver's side. Barely speeding in the left lane, heading down the highway toward another place in the state of North Carolina. Every Saturday for the past year and a half, Carter and I would get up early and drive until we found our place and just explore it. An abandoned old hospital, a brand-new hotel, the old private docks, we've been to them all. It all had value to us.

"We can't keep driving around forever, you know." he said with a grin on his face. It was just barely sunset and there was no place we thought was worth going to outside of town.

"Well then help me come up with ideas." I said mockingly.

"I already did, Beverly County."

"The place where you almost got bit by a rat? I don't think so." I laughed, sticking my hand out of a crack in the window, the wind slipping through my fingers.

"*You* thought it was a rat! It could have been anything. Also, I could have died and you would have just been standing there," he said.

"Yeah, yeah. You're a big boy."

I looked at Carter then in the dim light of the streetlamps, the lights and the shadows masking his appearance. Carter always drives. I refuse to get behind the wheel. I'm tired all the time and everyone else is mostly stupid.

He's got one hand on the wheel and his other arm resting in an L shape on the edge of the window that can't be opened. The knuckles on his left hand graze against the top of his car lightly. He's humming softly to some song on the radio that I don't know. His brown hair falls gently across his face and he grins widely, his jean jacket and forest green eyes forcing me to smile back. He still has his dimples but his freckles aren't as abundantly displayed across his cheeks as they used to be. He looks at me suddenly with a glint in his eyes.

"Hey, I know where we can go."

I rolled my eyes and chuckled softly. "I know that look. Carter, I am so sick of Taco Bell please God don't take me there ever again."

"Ok first off, I will never stop loving shitty tacos; and second, that's not where we're going. It's a place we never really go to."

"Oh, yeah right. What is it?"

He scoffed. "Like I'm gonna tell you after you just insulted the world's greatest authentic taco chain."

"Don't ever say that again." I warned, pointing at him threateningly.

He laughed.

"You really don't like our Taco Bell dates?"

"No, I do." I said, rolling my head in his direction and smiling guiltily.

A few minutes later we pulled up in front of a sandy spot beneath some tall and hollowed out tree. The same cool night, but a different feeling swelled up in the air. Just us surrounded by some ill-lit shacks of houses.

Carter turned the key in his ignition and hopped out of his car. I reluctantly stepped out of the passenger side and scanned the dark horizon. We were in a residential area of slightly dilapidated homes. It wasn't that late but there was almost no one outside save a man on his front porch.

"Where are we?" I asked, wrapping my thin jacket around my shoulders. I looked up at the moon and smiled.

"Just follow me." he muttered, already making his way into the small wooded area in front of us.

I ran to catch up with him through a narrow trail in a break in the trees and looked down at my sneakers, grimacing slightly as the feeling of soft ground began to catch beneath my feet. The trail changed from gravel and dirt to sand as we walked more.

I groaned. "Carter, I hate the beach." The beach is messy and complicated and I'm afraid of the mystery of that deep gray water. I haven't gone in since I stepped on that sharp coral that ripped some skin off my foot.

The one good thing about the beach that I have to admit is the sunsets, the sunrises too. Each new day and night a completely different work of art from the previous, the color palette changing in vast ways. The artist chose a vibrant orange and pale blue for tonight's viewing. It really was lovely. I just really hate sand. "I know. So do I."

He laughed and bumped his shoulder against mine, sniffing in the salty dew exaggeratedly through his nose. He held open his arms and let the wind throw his hair across his face, puffing out his chest dramatically. "Poseidon-come forth and awaken the love of the sea in me!"

I smiled and leaned on him as we made our way across the dunes and the waves came into view.

"Ok, so why are we here then?"
He put his arm across my shoulders and mumbled into my hair. "Because I love to see you miserable."

I rolled my eyes. "Really."

"Well, I don't know. I'm trying to fall in love with it I guess, since we live so close. Might as well, you know?"

"Yeah. That was a really dumb thing to say." I said, only half-joking.
He pushed me and ran ahead, I followed behind out of spite.

"How'd you even find this place?" I yelled after his retreating figure.

"Luck."

He waded in through a small tide pool and motioned for me to follow. I rolled my eyes and wondered why I put up with him.

"Come on!"

I stepped around the small pool of water slyly.

"God, you're so stubborn."

We walked up towards the shoreline, letting the waves tickle our toes. I wrinkled my nose as he waded in further and I shuffled in the water reluctantly, letting the cold water run across my shins.

"It's too cold Carter get out of there."

"But it is my destiny! I must become one with the ocean!" He said, splashing the water wildly around himself.

"Fine you wore me down, let's go to Taco Bell."

"Nope. We're too far in now. Too late to go back."

I groaned as he stepped towards me.

"Don't even think about it."

"Think about what?"

He smiled guilty and lowered his arms down to his sides.

"If you do this your car will smell like salt and death for weeks. Or, worse, a megalodon could swallow us."

"Megalodons don't exist. And even if they did, they would not be able to swim in two feet of water."

"You and I both know that's not-TRUE!"

And on that little word he picked me up and ran into the ocean, kicking up salty water all over us. I screamed and he laughed and people stared. He dropped me in and I sunk to the bottom, inhaling half the ocean in my struggle to the surface.

Finally, I swam to the top and sucked in air, standing quickly with a handful of sand in my palm.

"Asshole!" I yelled between gasps of air, scanning the water for him with my arm behind my head. He was floating on his back yards away peering up at the sky. I dropped my hand and walked over, shaking my head. He was always one for being dramatic, always wanted people to stare and wonder. Flip a switch and he could be a completely different person.

I came up behind him and plopped the handful of sand on his chest.

"Hey, this is a new shirt."

"Oh, ok. Like that matters anymore."

Carter scoffed and looked back up at the stars.

"Whatcha looking at?"

"Not looking. Just thinking."

"About your oceanic destiny?" I suggested.

"No. The prophecy has sadly already been fulfilled by Percy Jackson."

I laughed and sat down next to him, the water settling just above my chest.

"I'm thinking about college." I pulled my knees in and watched his breath dance up towards the sky.

"College? Don't start with that already, it's Summer."

"I know, I know. It's just a weird feeling." he replied, running his hands around us through the water. "I've lived in the same house on the same street in Alliance for my whole life. And suddenly in the blink of an eye, I can just leave it all behind, just like that. It's just weird and--I don't know."

"Yeah, I know. People do it all the time though. It's just life. Besides, you're gonna go to Appalachian. That's not too far."

"If I get in."

I laid down next to him in the water, letting the gentle sway of the waves pull us together.

"Do you ever think about college?" Carter asked, his green eyes acting as a mirror for the moon

"Of course I do. But I don't like to dwell on it, you know? I mean I don't want to spend half of high school worrying about something that's meant for the future. I'd rather live how I want now and worry about where it gets me later."

He locked eyes with me and sat up, pulling me towards him and letting me sink into his chest

I swallowed nervously, trying to conceal my surprised expression. "Are you about to kiss me? Cause that's disgusting and I will resist."

"Damn, too bad." he whispered, his eyes lingering on mine.
Dang it.
He put his chin on my head again and we looked out at a cruise ship
that was passing way out past our temporary part of the ocean. The
lights so far and so bright. Like a collection of human-made stars.
"I like the beach." I whispered to myself.
We got in his car with our soaking wet clothes and he drove me home,
singing along to The Shins the whole way back.
"So, same time tomorrow?" he asked as I grabbed my purple
bag out of the back seat.
"Can't. I have work."
"Yeah, so do I."
"Yeah, but unlike you, I actually care about my job." I teased,
punching him on the arm. He grinned back at me.
"Hey, I care. Rosie and I have an understanding."
"An understanding that she should fire you?"
"Exactly."
I rolled my eyes and stepped out of his car and into the road,
closing the door of his car behind me.
I walked around to my driveway and lingered outside, waving
goodbye as he pulled away. I watched him drive down the road
towards his house and wondered if he was looking at me through his
rear-view mirror, wanting to turn back around, pick me up, and just
drive. He had a way of making me feel like that.

2.

<u>September 26, 2017</u>

I broke my arm. It wasn't that bad, it was already half healed a month in. The cuts and bruises *almost* nothing more than a memory. I was lucky. People are always lucky. I try not to think about that.

"Why the mountains?"

My mom was driving. Something she hated doing. My dad was working so it was just her and I coming home from my therapist's office. Cars rides were so much different now, less exciting and more anxiety-inducing.

"Why not? The air is so fresh up there. You can clear your head. Get back on track."

"The air is the same everywhere mom, it's all recycled." I replied with a scoff.

"Well if heat rises, the good air must rise too."

I tapped a fingernail gently on the window and looked out across the hilly and green skyline before the long line of cars speeding down the highway. It's barely been more than a month.

"That makes no sense."

"I'll ask Dr. Lupa. See what she thinks about it."

"Sounds good."

The first time I saw my psychologist Dr. Lupa I spent more time quoting Star Wars than actually talking. It took her halfway through my second appointment for her to catch on. Needless to say, she was not happy with me.

Psychology is a pointless field to me. It's *my* brain, I know what I'm thinking you don't have to tell me. I know I'm depressed right now. I don't need a tiny woman with sharp eyes and a stress ball obsession to tell me that. Wasting my time by merely repeating what I say, scrutinizing every measly word. It's exhausting; I'm drowning in that long hour. It makes it worse when I sit still; no job, no friends, no future. With all that I am right now, college seems more distant and impossible every day.

"I feel like you're not listening to me."

I blinked and slowly lifted my head from the armrest, shaking myself out of my self-pity party.

"What?"

"Exactly."

I licked my lips and ran my hands down the front of the dash, feeling the stitching of the airbag beneath.

"I'm tired."

"I know. You've been tired for weeks."

I shrugged. "Guess it's time to start drinking coffee then. Or crack or something, whatever works."

Martha pursed her lips and shook her head, riding the brake like a nervous old woman. "You can't drink crack. I think."

She looked at me and sighed.

"It doesn't have to be like this, you know."

I peered at her questioningly. "Like what?"

"Hard. It doesn't have to be hard. You've got people trying to help you. You've been seeing Dr. Lupa for weeks now and still you act like a zombie. I hate seeing you act like this, but I can only do so much Dylan.

I rolled my eyes and sat up higher in my seat.

"Oh, you're right. I forgot, my life's great. My best friend's dead, my other friends all hate me, because, like you just so kindly pointed out, I'm a real bore. Not to mention, my doting mother is an alcoholic. I should really be more grateful."

"Hey, stop it, I'm your mother." She glanced sideways at me annoyedly and sighed. "And I didn't mean that zombie thing. You're just...angry and sad a lot more than you used to be."

"Really? Wow. That's so strange because I feel completely fine mom. I am so happy with the way things are going right now."

"Oh, are you serious? Again with the sarcasm. It's not funny, Dylan! I'm not laughing."

"I'm laughing."

"Really? It's been so long I forgot what your laugh sounded like."

"Right."

I crossed my arms and slouched in my seat again.

I sighed as a bright red stop sign passed slowly by the window. "You just ran a stop sign mom."

"Oh hush I didn't see a stop sign."

"Well it's been there for, like, ten years so I'm not sure how you missed it."

She sighed and I smiled. She really was a horrible driver.

"Someone's in a bad mood today." she mumbled.

I shook my head.

"Whatever happened with Kaylee and Maya? Haven't seen those girls in a while."

"They hate me now mom, we've been over this like a thousand times. We stopped hanging out my freshman year." Her smile wavered. "Their friendship was a real bummer anyways."

"They don't hate you and I'm sure that's not true." she said.

"Which part?"

"What part?"

I sighed. "Never mind mom. Let's just focus on your driving so we don't speed past a cop. Speed limits' 35 through here just so you know."

"I know, I'm barely speeding."

"Ok." I sighed.

We pulled into the driveway just before dinner. The sun setting above the rusty tin roof of our house like a halo on a trashcan. Rednecks roaming the streets with hefty thighs and small grimaces on their stretched faces.

I trudged inside the house, throwing my backpack on the ground and stepping out of my shoes immediately.

I heard the sounds of Fox News on in the living room and the dishes being passed in the kitchen. I made my way past the family portraits with forced smiles hanging up in the hall and towards the sound of talking in the kitchen. My dad and my older brother Sam sat at the table eating what looked like some burnt slabs of chicken and rice. I nodded at them and went to grab a plate off the counter.

"We're home." I sang, dropping a spoonful of rice onto my plate. I picked off a piece of burnt skin off the chicken and went around the counter towards the table, sitting in between Sam and my dad.

"Damn it, where's the remote Paul?" We barely turned our heads in the direction of Martha's voice.

She was simultaneously staring at the tv while throwing the couch cushions on the floor. I couldn't see the tv but I heard the sound of a movie commercial playing. I rolled my eyes and picked up my fork.

My dad turned in his chair and shook his head, chewing a piece of chicken loudly. "I don't know babe." he said between bites. She reached into the couch cushion and pulled out the remote, angrily hitting the off button, then throwing the remote back on the end table. "I swear to God he's taunting me." She said, storming into the kitchen.

"He's not, you're just obsessed," I suggested as she took a seat across from me.

My mom used to date this super hot guy in college before she dumped him for my dad. Daniel Pitts. You may have heard of him. The guy ended up staring in this huge movie that blew up a few months after they dated. I'm convinced she married my dad out of spite.

Martha glared at me as she started to cut the chicken on her plate.

"So kiddo, how was it?" My dad asked, trying to change the subject.

I stabbed the chicken monstrosity with my fork and crinkled my nose. "It was so much fun. Can't wait to go back next week."

My brother scoffed. My mom scooted in her chair across from me.

"Now, honey, don't start again." She said sternly. I saluted her as we all continued eating.

"Dr. Lupa says she's doing good, she's a lot more open to talking now," Martha added.

"Talking about herself or Star Wars?" Sam suggested with a smirk.

I grinned at him and shook my head.

"A little bit of both."

"You know, we don't have to talk about this stuff at dinner," my dad interjected.

"Ok," I agreed. There it is.

"How's your arm feel?"

I looked down at my left arm. It felt weird not having the cast anymore. "Better, thanks."

My dad nodded and went back to cutting the chicken on his plate. My family isn't that close but my dad has always been the outlier. Constantly asking questions and trying to avoid arguments. I never understood how he does it.

"Sam, what about you? How are things going at your internship?" he asks with a small smile.

My brother dropped his fork on his plate. An odd sort of smile fell on his face. He always did love talking about himself.

"It's going well. I thought waking up at 5 am to go work for some snobby rich guy halfway across town would be horrible but I actually feel good about it. Like today, we got to listen to some former homeless guy talk about how he lost his job as an accountant at, get this, Ernst and Young," he continued, gesturing with his hands throughout.

I nodded and pretended to listen. I pushed my food around my plate and tried to drown out the words being thrown across the table. Friendly chit-chat with the family always felt so uncomfortable to me. So unnecessarily friendly and awkward.

"Dylan?" my mom said suddenly, shaking me out of my thoughts.

"Yes." I stated matter of factly.

"Did you see it?"

"See what?"

"UNC's application. It opened a week ago. Are you going to apply soon?"

"Um yeah, yeah. I was thinking about maybe applying regular time now. I'm not even sure if I want to go there so why apply early, you know?"

"Well, I think that applying early can only ever help you. Sam can help you start it after dinner." she commanded, picking at her chicken with a frown etched on her face.

"That's ok, I can do it myself." I said, stabbing a bite of something on my own plate and chewing loudly.

Martha stopped cutting the slab of chicken on her plate and paused. I knew exactly where this was going.

"Are you sure you're actually going to do it?"

"Yes, I said I would." I asserted with an annoyed tone.

"Well, your word doesn't always mean much around here," Martha mumbled under her breath.

"You know I'm sitting right across from you, right?"

My dad intervened, shaking his head at us both. "No, she didn't mean that. Sam's filled that thing out before, I'm sure you'll need help on some things."

Martha pushed her chair back and went towards the fridge, searching frantically for her bottle of white wine.

"Really, I can figure it out. I'm sure it's not rocket science."

"No, it's college." my mom grumbled, pulling out the long thin bottle and pouring it gingerly into a glass

"Yes. Let me do it myself."

There was a moment of awkward silence. My mom cleared her throat and walked back to the table, the glass of wine in her hand spilling over the sides as she walked.

"What are you going to put on there for the summer anyway, avid dog walker and tv binge-watcher?" she mumbled.

I slammed my fork down. "Seriously?"

"Sam had two internships in less than three years, he had a job, and he volunteers at the study lab downtown. *That's* what colleges want to see."

I looked at Sam for some help. He shrugged in response.

"Are we really doing this right now? Better walking dogs than drinking myself blind. I can't deal with this right now." I pushed myself away from the table and rushed towards the door.

"I'm just trying to be realistic Dyl. Dylan!"

I slammed the front door and stomped down the steps of the porch, despite my lack of shoes. The shouts of my family meant nothing as I stomped out towards the garage. My bike was leaning against it. The sun was just setting and the street was lit only by the streetlamps on the sidewalks.

"Where you going in such a hurry kid?"

The porch light on the house next door shone down on my neighbor Ida. She was outside drinking wine on her porch, sprawled out across some old hickory rocking chair, her hand cupping the glass like a scepter. Her thick red glasses covered half her face and she had a wonky smile like she'd been drinking since 5. She looked like she stepped out of some magazine from the nineties.

"Good evening Ida. I am going on a nice bike ride to a less crappy area of town."

Ida laughed, her head rolling back exposing her long freckled neck.

"I'll drink to that kid," she vouched as she attempted to chug her whole glass of wine, spilling half of the liquid on her white shirt as she did. "Damn it. It looks so much easier when your mom does it."

I shook my head and grabbed my bike from the side of the house, quickly walking it down the length of the driveway.

"You always know what to say don't you Ida?"

"It's what I'm here for kid."

3.

Before

Before things went south, I used to work at an old Denny's knockoff by the water called O'Malley's. It's a short and wide building with a bright blue sign and contrastingly dull brown walls. I applied practically the day after my birthday so I could start saving for college or, as I should really put it, start spending it on stuff like second-hand jean jackets and candy from the drug store. Being a teenager has its perks. I worked there for exactly a year, which is pretty long considering the high turnover rate.

I never really got the hang of O'Malley's. The menu was complicated, the customers were impatient, and we were horrendously understaffed so it always seemed like we were in the middle of a rush even if there were only two tables there.

Other than a phone call, there was no real interview. They practically hired me on the spot. I turned in an application to the guy at the register who had already quit by the time I started.

My first day of work was a sad Tuesday in the fall of my sophomore year. I expected at least a week of training. Instead, I got a five-minute pep talk from the manager, Pete, to just smile and take all the insults they throw at me. Apparently, Pete's dad was the manager before him so he got the position by default. No one really wanted it anyway.

My first table was a family of six with allergies to everything on Earth. No gluten, no soy, no peanuts, and no carbs please.

There are no menu items that do not contain 100% of all of those things. They reluctantly ordered a plate of nacho cheese fries. When I came out of the kitchen with the steaming pile of cheesy goodness they had already left. They left five dollars on the table, which wasn't enough to cover their drinks, and a note that complained about how horrible I was.

I went in the back with the plate of fries and sucked on my teeth for a while, asking myself why anyone needed a job anyways.

"Yeah, they're all like that," a man said to me, setting down a heavy tray of dirty dishes into the sink. "I'm Carlos by the way." I nodded at him, staring up at his forehead. Carlos has thick black eyebrows that wiggle every time he talks. It's hard to not stare directly at them. He was always nice to me, despite his disdain for being a dishwasher at the worst diner in North Carolina.

"Dylan." I responded, setting the plate awkwardly in my lap.

"Dylan, huh? That's new. For a girl name, I mean."

"Yeah." I half grumbled.

"Sorry, sorry. Sure you never heard that one before."

I laughed and shook my head. "It's fine." I assured him, chewing on my lip. "So, do they all really just leave like that?"

"Not all of them. Some choose to wait to cuss us out beforehand or demand a refund before they leave. Those guys are just polite I guess." He said amusedly, his right brow twitching sporadically.

"Maybe I should quit while I'm ahead, right?"

Pete turned to us from the cash register, his small apron straining to cover his big stomach. "Please don't."

I put my hands up defensively. "I'm won't, I swear."

The door to the main floor swung open. A woman with long brown hair tied into a low ponytail came by with a tray of dirty dishes and plopped them in the sink. Her hoop earrings were almost as big as the pancakes she dumped into the trash.

"Not yet anyway, it gets to us all after a while. I'm Sawyer by the way," she beamed, extending her hand. Sawyer was my shift supervisor, a beautiful woman only a couple years older than me that worked to pay for Cosmetology school. She always said stuff like, "don't be like that, sugar," and "I feel like I'm riding on empty." A real country mom presence in the grunge den.

"Dylan."

"It's a pleasure to meet you Dylan," she replied, wiping her hands off on her smock. Pete eyed Sawyer with a frown and walked slowly into his office, shaking his head.

"Oh come on," Carlos sighed, moving to begin washing the mountain of dishes. "We only have, like, five tables. Why so many plates?"

"The people want what the people want. And right now, they want 4 extra plates with their entrees so they can all share." Sawyer said as she took a tube of cherry Chapstick out of her pocket and slathered it onto her lips.

Sawyer made her way out towards the floor again with a small notebook in her hand, tucking the tube of Chapstick back in her pocket. "Love your name by the way."

4.
October 1, 2017

"I remember before we'd used to stay up late in his room talking about how we'd want to die. A little morbid but, you know, as a teenager it just seems so far away. Anyways, I'd always say quickly in my sleep or something super mundane and then he'd say something completely opposite. Fighting off a bunch of zombies or getting lit on fire by some guy in a clown mask. He was weird like that."

It was 4:00. I sat huddled up on the couch in my therapist's office swaddled lovingly by a baby blue blanket and wearing my purple hat low on my head. A purple baseball cap, the color of bruises. Carter gave it to me. I felt like it was something lucky, so I wear it every day instead of trashing it like my mom so clearly wants.

Dr. Lupa is a matter-of-fact woman, 100% by the book. With her pointy nose and holier-than-thou attitude, she is the poster child of snobbery. I'm never really sure if she's trying to help me or lecture me.

"And when you both had those talks about- death- did things ever seem real?"

"What?"

"Was the subject of self-harm ever brought up?"

"No-no." I bit my lip to keep from snapping at her. "I'm just talking. There is no hidden meaning behind that. Carter may have been a bit moody at times but he was never suicidal."

"Are you sure?"

"Yes. That car hit *him*, Dr. Lupa. Not the other way around." Silence, hums of disapproval, writing. God that's so annoying, she can't just say what she's thinking out loud she has to write it all down and analyze it till it's limp and irrelevant.

"How's work going for you?"

"Oh, I thought I told you. I had to quit my job last month." I air quoted as I said quit. It was really more of a volunteered leave.

"Oh yes, I remember now. Would you like to speak more about that?"

"I just needed to get some things off my plate. Working was just another thing I had to stress about, what with all the horrible customers and all." I related, my thoughts lingering on a particular incident.

"Hmm."

"The leaking air vent in the back probably wasn't good for my health either."
Dr. Lupa managed a small smile and wrote something down again.

"Always have loved that snarky sense of humor you have Dylan. I'm glad you haven't lost that part of yourself."

"Yup." I stared down the clock on the wall on the opposite side of the room, watching the little hand tick slowly by.

"Your mother mentioned to me that you may have been experiencing some intense emotional spells, is that correct?"

"Um, you mean like telepathy?" I questioned facetiously. Dr. Lupa wiggled her painted toes and shook her head.

"Not quite. I mean having emotional breakdowns."
My face reddened slightly and I pulled the blanket tighter around myself.

"Oh, ok. Well, um, sometimes I get a little angry. I might leave the house for a few hours to cool down. But that's just normal stuff, right?"

"Ok. Well if there ever is a time where you feel it's something more, don't be afraid to let me know."

--

I narrowed my eyes as my mom pulled up seventeen minutes late in the car and shambled in, lowering the rim of my hat over my eyes.

"How did it go?" she asked.

"Good." Things were always just good. She nodded and continued talking, complaining about some woman at the grocery store and how my hat didn't make sense.

I pursed my lips as we got closer to home. "Did you tell Dr. Lupa that I've been having emotional breakdowns?"

My mom turned to face me with a slightly embarrassed look on her face.

"What? I mean, I thought she wasn't supposed to tell you stuff like that."

"Stuff that is about me?" I replied, feeling my voice begin to rise.

"Don't you think it'd be a good idea to tell her about stuff like that? It's her job to help you work through those things."

"I know but it's just that I don't really think I have breakdowns per se- I just get a little angry sometimes and I freak out a little."

Martha stared at me blankly. "Isn't that what a breakdown is?"

5.

Later that day

I swung my leg over the seat of my faded blue beach cruiser and pedaled. This is real therapy people. Riding down the street on a beach cruiser towards anywhere you want, in direct contact with the air and the world. I rode down my street half-asleep, half wide-awake, letting my memory guide me around the deep cracks and potholes in the road.

I looked up above me at the large and cascading canopy trees that lined my street. Thin strips of sunlight gleamed in towards my face. I pedaled on past the dusty old houses and street-parked cars. Carter hated street-parking, always afraid of someone scratching his horrible car. He didn't care that it was some used Camry, it was his. I pushed past those memories and pedaled on past all the brightly colored houses and half-empty streets.

Standing up on my pedals, I bent my elbows towards my ribcage and leaned as far as I could over the handlebars, picturing myself in the arms of DiCaprio on a huge unsinkable ship. My eyes lingered on a familiar street that seemed to go on forever. I felt a lump in my throat form as I pedaled past it.

I sat down again as a car approached and made a hard-left turn towards civilization. At the end of the road there was a strip mall and past that, a highway out of this place. I slowed down as the back of the small strip mall came into view. A nail salon, Romano's deli, a laundromat, and Rosie's Roller Rink. I pushed back on the pedals of my bike and put my toes on the ground to steady myself. I hadn't been down here in what felt like a long time.

Breathing deep, I settled beneath the last good tree on the street with some decent shade. My gaze lingered on the roller rink and I debated whether or I should go in. It was a small and decayed looking building in the middle of the strip mall. It had murder scene potential but the happy paintings of kids skating on the windows made it better. Or maybe worse. The little LED sign on the entrance read open. Carter worked there for four years.

6.

Before

We swerved around the small rink over and over, occasionally one of us tumbling over the heels of another. Mostly Carter over mine. He's bad at skating, he really sucks at it. I shielded the hyperactive disco ball from my eyes as I lent a hand to help him up again. "Break My Stride" tumbled out of the stereo and made my ears numb.

"Good God Dylan, watch it." Carter yelled jokingly as he stumbled across the rink.

"You're not British, Carter, stop pretending."

"Sorry, your skating skills really bring out the Englishman in me." he replied as he crouched down and looked up at me with a raised eyebrow.

"That makes no sense." I knelt down and pushed him forward. He protested amusedly as I watched him heading straight for the wall and face plant on the floor.

"Oops." I sang as I skated over to help him up.
Carter adjusted his T-shirt and steadied himself against my shoulder.

"Are you even allowed to be doing this?" I asked breathlessly above the music.

"Rosie isn't here. So, yes."
After school on particularly slow days, I saw Carter at work. It was only about a mile or so down the road from his house.
Rosie was the manager there and had a soft spot for younger Carter. That and no one wanted to work here because of its status as a former hideout for some people from the mob. So she hired him even though it was technically illegal at the time, paying him cash under the table until he turned 16.

"Hey, your birthday's in like a week." I shouted over the music, watching as Carter tried to skate forward with one of his legs out. It didn't work.

"Oh yeah. Almost forgot."

I rolled my eyes. "So, what are we doing?"

Carter shrugged. "I don't know. Figured I'd just wing it. Spontaneous birthdays are always so much better than the planned out kind."

"Of course you'd say that. At least brainstorm a few ideas." I suggested.

"Well, how about I drive over to your house at 4 A.M., I climb up to your window and knock until you finally wake up," he continued, stumbling multiple times on his skates. "Then we'll drive to the edge of town and climb Laurel Hill and have a picnic just as the sun is rising."

"You'd wake me up at 4 A.M. just so we could watch the sunrise? Why not just wait until night?"

"Hmm, not as spontaneous. This is just the first draft anyway. There's still the whole rest of the day I have to plan."

I relented and watched as he skated slowly around me, holding onto my shoulders for balance.

"Why do you work here if you're so bad at skating?"

He looked at me incredulously.

"Bad? I'm the best there is baby. Look around you!"

He gestured wildly and sped around me, falling on his butt like an incredible idiot. I laughed and bent down to help him up again as the other six people there rode around us with blank expressions. He pulled on my arms and I fell down next to him. A look of surprise fell across my face and I punched him on the arm.

"Oh my God. You really are just the best, aren't you?" I shouted.

We sat beside each other with our arms stretched out behind us and looked out at the other people on the floor.

"Jesus, I don't understand how people can look so angry at this place. It's funny seeing their faces with such severe expressions while the disco ball is going." Carter said.

"Yeah. This building has been known for attracting various murderers and lonely older men."

"Hey, I've heard that too."

"Well, that's who I'm here for. Don't scare 'em, away." I replied jokingly.

"Oh, is that why you're hanging out with me?"

"Wait, you're a murderer?"

"No, but I am over the age of 60 and looking to get some." Carter said, wiggling his eyebrows at me.

"Well you're in luck then." I said as I pushed myself back up on my feet with my hands.

"Am I ever. Let's do this right now, Matthew Wilder really gets me going."

He tried to stand but fell again and I skated past, blowing my bangs out of my face.

"Ok but really, you're terrible."

7.

<u>Present</u>

I stared at the roller rink for a few minutes and left. I didn't need another reminder of how much things had changed. Ever since that day ten years ago at the block party, he had always been there. There to listen. There to speak. Even there to just be. Lying face down on my bed while we both just talked at each other. That was all I needed.

I have these memories of him as a kid, playing with a bright orange ball in my backyard, throwing it at my feet to try and get me to play. His hair curly and messy, his smile wide and toothy. One of those poster children from, I don't know, Pottery Barn? Do they even have kids in their magazines? I don't know.

The point is, he was that rosy-cheeked, perfectly freckled kid you want to grab when you see them at the grocery store stealing the magic markers. He was my best friend.

The love I felt for him blinded me of anything else. I couldn't see my future, I couldn't see my past or present. I only saw his green eyes and wide smiles.

A bright light approached from behind me and I heard a loud wailing noise, reminding me that I was still real and should pay attention. I swerved my bike to the edge of the road and sucked in air rapidly from the back of my throat, the sudden action forcing me to fall off my bike and onto the pavement. A large gust of wind blew past me as a car flew by with the brights on.

"Shit," I mumbled as I watched him pass. I sat on the edge of the road and watched as he turned down the street, rubbing my bruised elbow gently. Slowly I lifted my body from the pavement and breathed deeply a few times, unconvinced that I had really been biking down the middle of the road for God knows how long. I stood up from the side of the road and picked up my bike. I assessed the damage that was done to my elbow, a small gash peeked out from under the sleeve of my t-shirt. Maybe just cool enough to be mistaken for a knife fight wound. I stood up and brushed the dirt off my shins and swung my leg back over, heading down the road toward where I was really supposed to be going.

--

I glided into the parking lot of a better-looking McDonald's but worse looking Denny's. O'Malley's, with the annoyingly bright purple and green LED sign to prove it. I leaned my bike against the back of the building and walked in through the front door. The smell of stale coffee grounds and greasy burgers drifted into my nose. I nodded at a lady I made awkward eye contact with sitting alone in a booth and reluctantly approached the bar. Sawyer popped up from beneath the counter and smiled at me widely with a look of relief.

"Oh my God Dylan. My baby girl." She put her spray bottle and dish towel down on the counter and swung around to give me a hug. She grabbed me and squeezed me tight and I hugged back. It was a good feeling.

"My God honey, it's great to see your beautiful face around here again. I'm about to go crazy with these boys let me tell you. Hey guys! Look who's here!"
I found myself quietly smiling and not knowing exactly what to say. Carlos and Pete came out from the back, each taking a turn peeking out from behind the swinging door before stepping into the cafe. It felt awkward being there, but also nice.

"Aye, Dylan," Carlos said, patting me on the back and going in for a hug.

Pete nodded at me and smiled, lingering awkwardly near the door. "It's great to see you, girl. What's up?"

"It's great to see you guys too, how has the store been holding up?" I asked.

"You know how it is, everything is shitty always. A woman literally barked at me yesterday. Barked." Carlos said as I stared at his forehead.

"Well, that sounds like fun."

Sawyer turned to me and put her arms around my shoulders. "How are *you* doing baby?"

I shrugged. "I've been better. Doing my best to finish this year and just be done with it. I didn't expect my last year here to be so disappointing."

"I hear that sister." Sawyer said, looking around at the store with a grimace.

I shrugged and stepped off the bar stool.

"Well, I came here to pick up my tips. You got anything left for me back there Pete?"

Pete's face fell a little at the mention of the safe and begrudgingly went in the back. Sawyer looked at me sadly and Carlos leaned over the counter with his lips pursed.

"So there's really no way you're coming back then?" she asked.

I shrugged. "Maybe one day I will, but not anytime soon. It's just not a good time."

Sawyer nodded and hugged me again, tighter than last time. "We understand, don't we Carlos?"

Carlos straightened slightly and walked towards us. "Well of course we do! And when you are ready, there are hundreds of greedy obese families waiting for you to take their order." I laughed and Carlos hugged me too. I could hear him sniff my hair and I rolled my eyes at Sawyer. Pete came out of the back and handed me a small wad of cash, all in dollar bills.

"Well, here you go. Sorry it's not much. You know the customers around here. Can't remember the last time I got a tip over ten bucks."

I nodded at him and flipped through the stack, eventually tucking it safely into my bag on my shoulder. I meant to leave right after that, but they offered me free juice if I stayed.

So I sat around with Carlos and Sawyer drinking orange juice from a ceramic mug at the bar for a while, each of us taking turns telling customer horror stories. After about an hour of messing around, a family sat down and Pete started eyeing us, I took that as my cue to leave.

"Well, I should get going. I hate biking in the dark down this road. The meth addicts really seem to love this part of town at night."

"Sure baby." Sawyer said, hugging me for a third time. "Come see us sometime. I'll give you any kind of pie you want for free."

I laughed as Pete shook his head and backed out of the restaurant towards his office.

Carlos held the door open for me and tipped his white hat. I tipped my own hat in reply. "Hey, can I give you a piece of advice before you go?" Carlos asked, putting his arm around my shoulders.

I nodded as we both slowly walked out the front door. "Sure."

"Disappointment is abundant in this world, Dylan. Don't take it personally. The world hates everybody. Take me for example. I wanted to be a stuntman. Instead, I'm a dishwasher at a glorified McDonald's." I smiled at Carlos and thanked him for the uplifting advice. The sounds of the deep fryer and a woman ordering veal encouraged me to get on my bike and ride far away before my dreams would suffer the same fate as Carlos'.

8.

<u>October 7th, 2017</u>

My mom sent me on a sandwich run to the deli by our house. She claimed she had a headache from too much white wine. I rode my bike there in the faded afternoon sunshine and my gray sweatpants. I pulled up in front of Romano's deli by the roller rink, lazily stepping off the seat, and winced as I felt the sun against my pupils. The mall was crowded with bikini-clad teenagers and wary new mothers. It felt weird having the strip mall be so crowded. Maybe it was a holiday.

I walked in the deli and stood in line behind a family clad in football jerseys, staring intently at the menu.

"Dylan?"

I stiffened and bit my lip. I hadn't heard the voice of someone my own age for a long time. I turned on my heel and found myself staring at a group of two similarly dressed girls. Kaylee and Maya. A pair of ex-friends that looked like they were made by Suffocation Crop Top Inc. Maya hugged me awkwardly, the takeout cup in her hand and my refusal to hug back make it really weird. Kaylee stood next to her with her arms crossed.

"Oh my God, how are you? I haven't seen you in forever!"

I nodded and looked down at myself in my stained Broncos t-shirt and gray sweatpants, drowning out half of what she was saying so I could focus on faking a genuine smile.

"Yeah, it's been awhile." I tried.

We stared. I heard the football jersey-clad family order behind me and hoped they would hurry.

"Well, how have you been? How's everything with that guy?"

Kaylee nudged her and cleared her throat.

"Oh. Yeah. Sorry. How are you with- everything?"

Oh great. Approaching conflict.

"I'm good. Just getting myself a sandwich or two."

Wow. My conversation skills are very limited.

I wanted to say I was doing the absolute worst ever and that she should leave before I scream at her or cry and punch something but I didn't think we were on good enough terms. I had barely seen them since sophomore year.

"Well, um, we're just about to go to the park and have a picnic or something. Do you want to join us?" Maya asked. Kaylee stiffened next to her but forced a smile.

I looked at their faces. And then at the family in line ahead of me. And then I thought, you know what, I would really like to get away from the house. Maybe things could still be normal between us three. Half-normal at least.

"I'd love to come."

Kaylee drove us a few miles into town to the park. I sat in the back and watched the cars go by. It was an awkward car ride, but I really always did love making things awkward. Kaylee has an obnoxiously red Mercedes Benz. I spent most of the ride listening to them talk about all the boys who wanted to screw them. Eventually, we pulled up to the park beside the city and we all piled out. They chose a picnic bench by the sidewalk, a prime gawking spot for any passerby wanting an eyeful of someone's ass.

"So where have you been anyway? I haven't seen you at school," Kaylee asked with a half-innocent look on her face.

"My parents decided it'd be a good idea for me to finish school at home. After everything."

"Oh God, I would hate that. Being home all the time, no social life. Being by myself all the time, or with my parents nonetheless. That sounds like the worst."

"Yeah, it's not as bad as you think. I can basically do whatever I want all day."

"Oh, that's cool. What about, like, parties and stuff? How do people talk to you?"

"Well I have a phone so they can just text me or call me or come to my house or something."

"That's a lot for just one person."

"Yeah well if they--it works out. Don't worry about me I manage just fine."

"Ok."

A man whistled as he walked by and the girls took a moment to giggle and pretend like they weren't expecting it.

"So, what have you guys been up to?"

"Oh my God, literally nothing. You haven't missed anything Senior year, Dylan. It's all the same shit as last year." Maya assured me.

"Yeah I literally want to kill myself my life is so boring right now." said Kaylee as she twirled a strand of her hair.

"What no you guys are so involved."

"I can't think of a single thing," Maya said as she chomped down on her sandwich, smearing lipstick all over it.

"Well, this thing actually happened yesterday. Last night, actually," Kaylee interjected.

Maya's eyes widened at the prospect of even a shred of gossip. Brown and blue, perfectly painted. Maya leaned in and smiled, a piece of turkey was stuck between her front teeth. "Oh my God, what happened? Did you and Nick finally hook up?" Kaylee laughed awkwardly and shook her head, a lock of velvety blond hair falling in her face.

"No. Never mind, it's nothing actually I shouldn't tell you." she spat. Maya looked at me and scoffed. "No way Kaylee you have to tell us now, what is it?"

"Yeah, just tell us," I urged mockingly, bringing my foot up to rest on the bench. Maya's eyes moved between my hat and my t-shirt, obviously debating whether or not she should tell me how ugly they are. I hesitated. *These* used to be my best friends.

"Ok fine, I'll tell you. But seriously don't say anything, alright?" she said, looking around the park and leaning over the table. "Brady and I sort of-hooked up last night."

Maya screeched with delight and I sat there nodding. My face reddened.

Brady Dean was your typical high school jock asshole. He lived in the same neighborhood as Carter and I and bullied us all throughout middle school.

"I know, his parents were away on business or something so he invited me over to hang out. Next thing I know, we're making out on his couch in the living room with his hand up my shirt. It was amazing."

"Oh my God Kaylee, I can't believe it. Brady Dean!" Maya said.

"Yeah, sounds real romantic." I mumbled under my breath. Kaylee struggled to laugh and nodded. "Yeah."

"When did you guys become a thing? Tell us everything!" Maya encouraged, leaning forward on the table with her elbows."

"Yeah. Everything." I said.

Kaylee smiled and pushed her sandwich to the end of the table with her finger.

"It just sort of happened. We always make eye contact in the hallway and I guess Jessica gave him my number or something because that's how we started talking. It was really nice, he's a great guy."

Maya nodded excitedly and I pursed my lips.

"It's kind of crazy to think that we've known Brady for almost, what is it, ten years? Chasing after us down the street with fireworks, opening up the door on us while we're in the bathroom, trying to kick me in the stomach in the hallway at school. What a great guy."

Kaylee stared at me and grimaced. "Yeah. That's the old Brady though, Dylan. He's changed since then."

"Oh really? He's changed since three months ago? Because I feel like I remember seeing him buying weed behind the gas station a couple days ago."

Kaylee sighed and blew air out of her nose. "Yes, I heard about that Dylan. I'm telling you, Brady's a good guy. Don't be such a downer." I nodded and took a bite of my sandwich, relishing the feeling of the uncomfortable air of the table. Kaylee grabbed her phone out of her bag and started texting. Maya stared at her sandwich and poked at it awkwardly.

"My therapist said I shouldn't see you." I blurted between bites of my Italian sub. A long pause ensued those vulnerable words. I thought that saying that would be more of a stinger but the longer I waited for the response, the more helpless and sad they sounded.

"What?" Kaylee sneered as more of a statement than a question. She dropped her phone on top of the table and leaned forward with a sneer. "Your *therapist* told you that?"

"Yeah."

"Why?" Maya asked timidly. I shrugged and stared blankly in her direction.

"I don't remember why exactly," I claimed, picking at a piece of bread stuck between my teeth. "Maybe it's cause you're both manipulative and controlling."

A little blue vein throbbed above Maya's left eye. "What the hell is that supposed to mean?"

I shrugged. "The drama, the bipolar attitudes, jealousy, all that." The vein bulged above her angry sea blue eyes. "Oh sorry, was that mean?"

"What are you talking about Dylan?" Kaylee asked. "Look, I know you've been through a lot but what you're saying is kinda bitchy."

"I'm glad they have the intended effect."

"Wait, are you just saying this cause you're jealous of me and Brady?"

I laughed. "Oh God no. Brady's a bully, he's probably the worst guy ever. So, I'm not jealous. I'm actually happy that two people have found their exact match."

Kaylee pursed her lips and crossed her arms, I could tell she was about to blow.

"Are you fucking serious? What the hell happened to you? I don't think you're hearing what you're saying to me right now."
I scoffed and rolled up the sleeve of my t-shirt. "There it is. That's the Kaylee I remember. Always so angry and pretentious. I mean for God's sake, you treated me like your little slave for the last four years. You can't just expect to order me around all the damn time. You're selfish and not at all who you used to be."
An unexpected jolt of the table made my halfhearted attempt at appearing unbothered by her words fail. My eyes flashed as she pushed the table harshly into my ribs. A sharp stab of pain crawled through my bones and settled above my stomach. I gasped harshly and coughed.

"You're fucking crazy. I'm not the bitch here, you are. You judge me all the fucking time and you constantly sit around your house alone and feel sorry for yourself. I've barely even seen you since freshman year because you became obsessed with that Carter kid. I'm done with these accusations, I'm done with this bullshit, I'm done with you. Don't get all angry at me when *you're* the one who ruined our friendship in the first place."
She motioned for Maya to get up and grabbed her purse off the bench.

"You know, I only invited you here because I felt sorry for you but forget it. You deserve all the pain you have coming at you."
I watched as they left, throwing away basically the whole sandwich they bought on their way to Kaylee's Mercedes. I stared off in their direction for a while and closed my eyes, letting the sun shine on my face until I felt warm.
The realization that I left my bike at the deli shook me out of that. I guess that means I'm walking.

I cut through some parking lots and got to the deli in a little under twenty minutes. I walked towards my bike and unhooked the lock from around the lamppost. My eyes landed on the roller rink and I stopped, really thinking about what Kaylee had said. I felt a sudden need to go in then. I had to go in.

I leaned my bike against the wall of the building, said a prayer that it wouldn't be stolen, and opened the door.

Instantly, an eerie feeling hit me. It wasn't fear, it was like getting lost in your own neighborhood. Nothing had really changed, I thought for some reason it would after three months.

It was always sort of dark in there. The lights were dimmed and the disco ball sent occasional flashes of round light across the floors and the walls and the everything. The small arcade by the snack bar, each thing more overpriced than the last. I walked down the stairs towards the place where you rent out skates but stopped when I saw a new sign out of the corner of my eye.

Turning on my heel, I saw it was a small picture of Carter on a corkboard when you first walk in the door. In loving memory. I put my finger on Carter's face and dragged it down to his lips. The print job on his picture was crappy, but his face was completely recognizable. I bit my lip and smiled down at the display of pictures taped onto the board and the small collection of flowers at its base. The employees had taped up all the pictures they had with him and wrote a note on each one. I looked at every picture with a sad smile. I squinted at one that I found up there with me in it. It was Carter leaning over the skate rental desk with his arms stretched out. I stood next to him laughing with a big foam hat on my head. Some random day last year. I shook my head and ran my finger up to that picture with a small smile on my face. I could barely make out the small gash on his head from falling off the dock the week before. The pictures-it was a small thing to do but somehow made my soul feel big. Just for a second.

"Dylan?" I turned my head, leaving my finger on the big picture of Carter.

It was Rosie. George was peeking his head out from the snack bar. He gave a small wave and ducked back in his booth.

I dropped my hand as Rosie came towards me with outstretched arms. She hugged me.

9.

Before

I left school early and ran to the park downtown. It's only about a mile away or so. I wanted an excuse to see him outside of school. Carter had left for a surprise trip to Atlanta two weeks ago and I had barely seen him since. I sat alone in a patch of grass and breathed deeply, letting my heart rate slow itself down. There was a small collection of stalls set up in the middle of the park with people selling things. The smell of fried dough and honeydew drifted over to my little island so I walked over and began to look. A hand tapped on my shoulder as I was looking at a local honey booth and I turned with a sample stick in my hand.

"You're early." I teased as Cater bumped me with his hip. He had his black sunglasses on and a pair of light wash jeans, despite the 80-degree weather.

"Wasn't about to let you skip without me." He picked up a wooden sample stick and squeezed some sort of spicy honey onto it, humming with satisfaction.

"Want some?" he offered, squeezing some more out of the bottle and onto the stick. He nodded at the woman behind the stall as he did it and she nodded back.

"No thanks." I said with a tight-lipped smile.
He grabbed my arm as I picked up a bottle of jam and inspected it.

"Hey, you ok?"

"Yeah. Just wanted to get you out of school."

We walked through and judged the stalls accordingly, buying two lemonades and a book about dying. He spread a blue blanket from his car across a grassy area and we both laid down on our backs, sipping and chewing on the straws of our lemonade and staring up at the sky. After a long period of silence, I looked back at him, wondering why he hadn't initiated any form of conversation yet.

"Whatcha thinking about?" I asked.

He turned and I squinted my eyes, the sun shining down harshly on us both.

"Nothing." he said as he sat up, shaking the grass bits out of his brown hair. It was shorter then.

"Come on. You've been acting weird all morning."

He looked away and shrugged. "I'm just thinking."

"What about?" I asked.

He opened his mouth like he wanted to say something but then shut it again. I pushed myself up on my elbows.

"Carter-are you ok? What's this really about?"

"I don't know. I don't know."

"Just tell me."

He pursed his lips and I felt him looking at me through his sunglasses, giving a defeated sighed through his nose. "TJ just got out of jail. That's why we were in Atlanta. He was caught with some pot in his car or something stupid. I don't know."

"Oh, my God. I didn't know that. Why didn't you tell me?"

He shrugged. "I don't know. I meant to but it felt weird to hear those words in my mouth. I mean TJ in jail? That doesn't seem right."

I nodded and sat up. "You're right, that doesn't seem like him."

"He says it wasn't him but no one really seems to care." He said, fiddling with the straw on his lemonade, his hair falling softly across his face.

"Well, I'm sorry, but you shouldn't beat yourself up about it. There's nothing you can do."

"Yeah, I know. I guess I'm just worried now about disappointing my mom. You know she's real pissed with what happened to TJ, my dad, the grands, everybody. I don't wanna be another thing she has to worry about."

"You're not, Carter. She's proud of you."

Carter stared out at the market. "It just doesn't make sense. I keep replaying the image of TJ in that jail cell. It didn't feel right."

"Of course it didn't. He's your brother. That'd be hard for anyone to see."

He looked down again at his feet, gently fiddling with his shoelace. I put on my hand on his back.

"What do you want me to say C? What can I say?"

"Don't say anything. Just sit here with me. Let me sit here with you." He continued as he laid his head in my lap. "Tell me how to get over it."

"Well, it's a simple concept," I assured as I stroked Carter's hair, trying to channel my inner soothing voice. I looked out across the market and struggled to find the right words. "Well, don't think about anything else but this moment. Think about this," I instructed, gesturing to the park in front of us. "Think about, um, senior year and how amazing this lemonade tastes. Think about me. Think about us."

He shook his head half-heartedly. "Ok. I'll try."

He grabbed my shoulders suddenly and laughed. "You should take some of your own advice you know Oprah."

I nodded. It was weird that day. With the roles reversed and everything, I mean.

"You know what I'm thinking?" he said suddenly, peering up at me through his sunglasses.

"What?" I asked, looking down at the stubble on his face.

"Let's go on an adventure to the docks."

"I like that idea."

10.

Later that day

The sky was a dusty blue, a silky lavender, a blush pink. I felt trapped in an oil painting looking up at it. Him and I at the base of the docks where the wealthy kept their boats in the hands of the worst security you've ever seen. So bad, even two scraggly teens could hop the fence without getting caught. We snuck nervous glances behind our shoulder nevertheless, making our way slowly down the dock towards the edge of the water. Taking off our shoes, we sat down at the end of the dock where the deck was clear and the air was the saltiest.

We sat alone with our feet in the water, watching the clouds collect like sponges above us. He stretched his long legs towards the ocean waves and swirling wind and I scooted closer next to him, laying my head on his shoulder. Wishing we had more time, wanting to say something meaningful. But what could I say? How could I have known?

It was a Tuesday but it felt like a Saturday. The day started to smell like roses and honeycomb as the morning bled into the afternoon. Suddenly he stood up, pulling his shirt over his head. I looked around the dock and then back at Carter.

"What are you doing?"

"It's hot. I'm gonna jump in." he said matter-of-factly.

"What? No, you're gonna get in trouble."

"No, we're not. We're already trespassing anyways. Come on."
He put his shirt down by his shoes and helped me up.
I sighed. "You don't know how deep it is."

"It's a marina. It's gotta be deep."
I stepped back and sat down on the tackle box behind me, folding my arms.

"Come on Dylan."

"No, I'm good." He looked at me with a raised eyebrow. I stared back unimpressed.

"Ugh, fine. I'll go in all alone I guess," he whined with an exaggerated frown.
He turned his back to me and ran towards the water, shouting wildly as the water flew around him in little droplets. I laughed at him and uncrossed my arms, leaning forward with my chin in my hand.

"Is it cold?" I asked as he pulled himself out of the water.
He ran his hand over his face, the water dripping off his clothes and forming a small pool on the deck. "Not too bad," he said as he came towards me again, pulling on the sleeve of my shirt and begging for me to jump in with him.

"No, this is my favorite shirt."

"Take it off."
I rolled my eyes and sat back down, feeling the blush make its way up to my cheeks. He smirked and ran backward, trying to show off his dock jumping skills. His foot caught on a rope and suddenly he fell, bumping his head hard on the edge of the dock and falling into the water with a small splash. I ran over to the edge of the dock and called his name, leaning into the water and scanning the area with a new accumulation of foam and bubbles. Carter. Carter. Carter.
Oh my God.

The water suddenly splashed into my face and he shot to the surface. A feeling of relief washed over me and I grabbed his arm, my heart beating wildly in my chest. He flopped down on the deck and I crouched down beside him.

"Are you ok?" I asked as he struggled to get into a kneeling position.

"I'm fine," he stressed. He was panting heavily and his face was flush. He turned towards the water again and threw up into the ocean.

"Oh God."

I went to my bag and dialed 911 on my phone, giving a vague description of our location. I gently asked if he was ok again and he nodded slowly, wincing as his head bobbed up and down. I took one of his arms and laid it across my neck, whispering encouraging words to him as we both hobbled slowly down the dock. The ambulance showed up within five minutes, just as we reached the entrance of the marina. A paramedic helped him climb into the back.

I rode with Carter in the ambulance as he groggily asked the paramedic stupid questions. A small spot of blood was oozing down his face. The hospital was a quick ride away, a small one by the shore. I shook my head at the sight of you splayed out across the small stretcher with your green eyes wandering across the ceiling. So much for staying out of trouble.

When they wheeled Carter in the back room, I put his stuff on a chair and picked up his phone, dialing the number of his mom reluctantly. I felt a bit bad having to call her after what he said at the park, but she's his mom. She had to know.

She showed up about 20 minutes after we talked briefly on the phone. I stood up nervously when she came in. She was wearing her work clothes.

"Hey Ms. Higgins." I stammered with a small smile.

"What happened?" she asked. It sounded more like a command than a question to me. Mrs. Higgins always had that sort of intimidating authoritative presence, in a motherly sort of way.

"The guy in the ambulance said it was probably just a concussion. Like I said over the phone, he tried jumping off the dock backward."

"The private dock you mean. You two jumped the fence?" she asked as she stood in front of me with her arms crossed.

"Yes. Do you wanna sit?"

She sighed. "Sure. Is that his stuff?" she asked, gesturing to the small pile of clothes I had on the seat.

"Uh, yeah." she took them in her lap and sat down, setting her purse down next to her and folding her hands in her lap, looking at the clock on the wall and then back at me. "Well. It's 3 o'clock now. I'm guessing you two skipped school again today too."

I rubbed my leg awkwardly. "Uh, yeah."

"Hmm. Perfect. Well, why'd you do that?"

"It was my fault Mrs. Higgins, I asked Carter to meet me at the park."

"I'm not blaming you, Dylan. He was the one that decided to jump in the water, right?"

I nodded.

"That's what I thought. One of my sons just got out of jail and the other is in the ER."

I shuffled awkwardly in my seat. "That's not your fault either."

"Doesn't matter. They're my kids, my responsibility."

I nodded awkwardly again and we sat in silence for a while.

We waited for a little over an hour when the doctor called us back. I sat there for a few minutes and let Mrs. Higgins see him first. She came back out shortly and nodded at me as she went out the double doors.

I was never sure where Mrs. Higgins and I stood. I imagine she thought of me as the little girl she knew from the block party that grew up to be a bad influence. I walked down the hall towards where Carter's room was.

I stopped in front of the thick tan door with the little paper plague that read *Higgins, Carter*. Very official. He was there alone- sitting on his bed and staring out the window at the highway. He didn't look too bad. There was a small bandage on his forehead and his eyes looked a little glassy. His brown hair was mused from the pillow and he was frowning a little.

I sat down next to him, breathing heavily. Just me and him.

"How you feeling?" I asked.

"Dizzy, thanks. I can't believe you forced me into the water."

I rolled my eyes and punched him on the arm as he managed a small smile.

"When can you leave?"

"Later tonight, my mom's gonna bring me some lasagna."

"Nice. You want me to stay 'til then?"

"You got anything better to do?"

I laughed and crossed my legs.

"Was your mom mad?"

"Not really. I think she's just glad I'm not in a jail cell."

I nodded guiltily. "Are you mad at me for calling her?"

He looked at me with a small smile. "Of course not. If you didn't, I would not be having lasagna."

I laughed and watched as he looked again outside the window, the room growing very quiet. I followed your gaze but saw nothing but the cars going past on the road.

"Do you remember that day at the beach last year when we swam out too far?" he said suddenly.

I looked at him questioningly. His face looked sad for a second.

"Yeah." I said. His eyes locked outside. His face blank.

"We went past the dock and the reef and all the way out past where the lifeguard said the sharks breed. You said you wanted to touch the bottom and punch a shark or something."

I scooted closer and nodded with an amused smile.

"I thought of something then. Super morbid. I could've drowned that day if I wanted. I could have easily smashed my head on a rock or something and be up listening to records with David Bowie."

"Don't say stuff like that-"

"But I didn't. I didn't want to." He moved his gaze to my face and his eyes softened slightly.

"That used to be the only thing I'd think about when I was younger. I had nobody."

"That's not true-"

"But not anymore. Because now I have you. And that's the reason I've never done it. Because I've got you and you've got me and that's the only kind of heaven I need right now."

I held his gaze and felt my eyes start to water a little. He was always a flirt. But he was never this sentimental.

I love you, I thought. I raised my eyebrow at him and smiled.

"I like that." was the best I could say.

"Well I like you." he replied cheekily.

I bit my lip and nodded.

"I like you back."

"Good." he said finally, his face breaking out of its state of sadness.

"You have a concussion." I said.

"I know."

We stared out the window again and I leaned on his shoulder.

"So while I was daydreaming about fighting bionic sharks, you were thinking about killing yourself?" I asked, half joking and half concerned.

"They were bionic? And no- I was examining the possibility. I wasn't gonna actually do it."

"Right."

"Don't be a smartass right now Dylan, we're sad."

"Sorry. Wait, why are we sad? Is it cause you're stupid and I was right?"

"Yes."

11.

September 15, 2017

I laid my bike against the back wall of O'Malley's and went inside. I was three hours early to my shift. I couldn't go home and I didn't want to go anyplace alone so I figured I may as well make some money.

I struggled to pull my smock over my head with the purple cast on my arm and then I went to clock in on the computer in the back. Carlos greeted me with a friendly smile by the sink. His face was red with heat, his black shirt soaked with sweat.

"Aye, Dylan! What's up girl?"

"Hey Carlos," I said eyeing his disheveled frame "I'm a bit early, do they need any help with tables?"
He shrugged and flung a dish towel over his shoulder.

"I don't think so. We've been pretty slow today."

"Ok, thanks." I said, punching in my passcode onto the small computer. I felt small beads of sweat already dripping down my back

"Geez," I said, grabbing a stray menu from a rack of dishes. "Why is it so hot back here?"
Carlos chuckled. "Air broke. Pete says he can't get it fixed 'til Tuesday."
I sighed and continued fanning myself with the menu, relishing the feeling of the cool air on my face.

"Oh wait," Carlos shouted suddenly as I moved to put my backpack down. He laughed excitedly. "Stay right there."

I looked at him amusedly and put my book bag down, pulling my apron on over my head and placing my hat on the coat rack. I sat down on the stool by the sink, looking down at the collection of dirty dishes. Carlos pushed open the swinging door with a piece of pie in his hand, balancing it carefully on a small white plate. Sawyer followed behind him with two other slices, eyeing him with uncertainty. She brightened suddenly when she saw me, setting down the pie on the foldable employees only table and coming in for a hug.

"Hey baby." She said as she rubbed my back.

"Hey Sawyer." I said with a chuckle.

"How's your arm doing?" she asked, gesturing to my cast.

I looked down at it and sighed. "It's fine. I'm supposed to be getting it off next week."

She nodded as we both began to fan ourselves with our hands.

"Don't worry," Carlos continued as he set his pie down, "This plate is actually really clean."

I shook my head as Carlos and Sawyer beckoned for me to have a seat at the table. "Wait, I'm confused, what is this for?" I asked as I hopped off the stool and towards the small table.

Sawyer and Carlos looked at each other and shook their heads. "It's your anniversary darling! Today marks a year since your first day of work."

My eyes widened slightly. "Geez, it's already been a year? How do you guys even remember that?"

Sawyer shrugged sheepishly. "Oh honey, we love celebrations," she continued, leaning in to whisper in my ear. "And the only time Pete ever lets us eat any of the pie is for a special occasion. So just go with it."

I nodded and smirked at them both. "Alright then. Thanks guys." I said as each of us dug our forks into the pecan pie and hummed with delight. We talked for a while and took turns cleaning plates. It didn't take long for the heat to encourage us to actually do our jobs.

I pushed the swinging door out to the hallway between the back room and the floor and nodded at Sawyer as she started cleaning behind the bar.

"You mind grabbing that table in the corner baby?" She asked gesturing to an isolated booth full of guys that looked about my age. They were wearing lettermen jackets and snickering loudly, hunching over the table and throwing little wads of paper at each other.

"Course not." I said reluctantly.

"You're an angel." Sawyer said as she emptied a pot of coffee grounds into the trash.

I walked around the edge of the bar and came up beside the table with a notepad.

"Hey welcome to O'Malley's. Can I get some drinks started for you?"

Six pairs of eyes all turned to me and I was met with the faces of the core jocks of Alliance High. Sitting closest to me was Brady Dean. One of the jocks tried to open his mouth to say something but Brady waved him off.

"Dylan? I didn't know you worked here." Brady began. He looked me up and down and readjusted his position on the booth, his eyes lingering on my cast.

"Yeah it's been a few months." I warily stepped further away from him.

"Oh. Hey, I'm real sorry to hear about Carter. He was a great guy."

"Yeah." I said with a frown. What an ass.

"So, what'll it be?"

They ordered their food and drinks at the same time. Football practice they said. I did not care.

I hung up their orders on the wire in the back and tried to stay away from the floor. It was hot in the back and I was nervously sweating. My sweat stains were very visible through my green shirt.

I walked out from the back room and through the bar to the hallway on the other side of O'Malley's, fanning myself with a menu as I walked. It was much cooler by the doors. I stood staring at the screen on the register and clicking random buttons to keep myself busy.

The sound of someone walking slowly down the hall forced me to look up from the register. It was Brady. I felt my eyes widen slightly but I kept my composure.

I smiled with my lips. "Bathrooms back that way," I asserted, pointing behind me.

He laughed and nodded, stepping towards me with his hands in his pockets.

"I know. Saw you back here. I wanted to talk."

I took a deep breath and backed up towards the wall. "You want to talk to me? Why?"

"I don't know. See how you're holding up. Is your arm ok?"

I folded my arms across my chest as he continued to walk slowly closer. "You're joking right?"

"No. You know, I feel real bad about how things went down between me and you and Carter."

I shook my head and scoffed. "Well, you're a couple months too late. If that's all you wanted to say you should probably leave because I don't accept your apology. Neither would he." I turned back towards the computer hoping he would leave.

There was an awkward silence while I went back to hitting random numbers on the keypad. I could feel my heart beat faster and faster in my chest.

"How's TJ?" Brady asked suddenly.

I turned my head slightly. "How do you know TJ?"

Brady was standing close to me so I turned all the way around. I looked around him at the wall and out at the cafe. I could just barely see one of the jock's heads. "We're friends," he suggested.

"What? What are you playing right now Brady?"

Brady took one of his hands out of his pocket and tucked a strand of hair behind my ear. I grimaced and slapped his hand away. He raised an eyebrow at me and took a step closer.

"If this is a joke Brady it's not funny. And if isn't a joke, it's still not that funny."

"I just wanna be friends, Dylan." He said in a low voice. I looked up at his face, his eyes sparkling and his stubble rough against his chin. He leaned in suddenly and I recoiled with disgust. I raised my foot in a rapid motion and Brady fell back as I kicked him hard against his shin.

I quickly ran out of the back room and through the bar towards where Carlos was working, not taking a second to look back. Sitting down on the stool in the back, I breathed hard and tried to go over what just happened. Brady was a real sleaze and there was no way I was serving him after that stunt. I claimed I was having an asthma attack so Sawyer would take their dishes out for me. I don't have asthma.

I sat back there for a long time letting the heat numb my brain. Sitting and basking in the humidity, I refused to leave the chair until Pete started eyeing me.

Straightening my apron, I went back outside, serving a table on the opposite side of the restaurant. I picked up a few full dirty dishes from another table and walked towards the backroom, balancing a particularly heavy dish on my cast. The sound of the jocks snickering followed me as I walked.

I felt something hard shoot out beneath me and the plates began to slip out of my hand. I tried to steady myself but ended up falling on the floor as my foot jammed itself underneath a nearby chair. I heard the sound of ceramic breaking and food falling everywhere as I face planted on the cold tile floor. The restaurant became quiet.

I slowly picked myself up off the floor and looked sideways at the foot I fell over. One of the jocks. I looked over at Brady's table and saw him laughing his ass off with his friends.

I stood in shock staring at the spaghetti and syrup medley that had accumulated on my chest. I didn't know how to feel in that moment. I dropped the only plate I had left in my hand on the ground and ran out towards the back door, the laughs and loud voices of the jocks pushing me away. I heard voices calling after me but I just left. I pushed open the exit door and instantly felt the tears falling down my face. It was only 5 o'clock and I already felt like crap. I sunk to the cool ground, breathing hard and letting the hot tears roll down faster and faster. I felt a little angry, then a little sad, like I was being suspended in the air and people were throwing rocks at me. I looked down at my shirt again and grimaced, picking off long strands of pasta with my fingers. The door opened and allowed the sound of loud yelling to reach my ears. Sawyer stepped towards me with a bleach stained towel in her hand. The door slammed behind her and she approached me with a sorry look on her face.

"Oh God, Dylan."

I averted my eyes and let her sit next to me. She handed me the towel and I nodded my thanks, lightly dabbing at my shirt even though it was really just making things worse.

"Kids are real jerks these days."

"Yeah, tell me about it."

"If it makes you feel any better, Carlos really showed 'em. Pete and Mario had to hold him back from trying to punch that guy."
I nodded.

"I think he's always had a bit of a crush on you."
I stared at the ground a little harder, kinda wishing she would just leave.

"Don't let it get to you baby. Those boys in there are bullies. It's got nothing to do with you."
Silence.

"What are you thinking Angel?"
I shook my head, feeling the hot tears pick up speed again.

"I'm thinking about my…my life right now. I thought things could never really get any lower than this," I whimpered gesturing to my sweat and tomato sauce covered shirt. "I really miss him Sawyer." Sawyer put her arm around my shoulders and stroked my hair gently, moving some stray brown locks out of my face. I rubbed my hand gently over my cast, tracing each person's handwriting with my thumb.

"I know baby. I know." she said as she kept stroking my hair and letting the tears fall down my face.

"I think I might quit."

12.

Before

It's nice out. The kind of nice that requires only a smile to be considered a perfect day. I wrap my thin red rain jacket around my body as I slam the door of my house. Sometimes I like to do that to wake everyone up and make them angry. Works every time. The sight of a pale Camry against the dreary backdrop of dead North Carolina oaks makes me feel warm inside.

"Well, good morning sunshine," Carter says with his wide grin as I slide into the passenger seat.

"Carter. Glad to see you really tried hard this morning." I smirked at his green pajama bottoms and patted him on the leg.

"Very funny Mom. Hey, is it supposed to rain today?" he retorted, pulling on the sleeve of my rain jacket. I punched him playfully on the arm.

"Hands on the wheel, jackass. You know this is basically my security blanket."

"Yeah, that's what I thought."
I shook my head and gazed out the mud caked window as he pulled out of my driveway.

"So, how are you feeling?" I asked. The windows inviting in the cool air as we sped off, the radio lazily singing the anthem of the dawning sky and small birds outside.

"Better, thanks. The pain is pretty much gone, the dizziness is still there sometimes though. I'm a little afraid to see how much work I have to make up."
I nodded and looked over at him. "You know, when you were in the hospital, you said some pretty crazy things."

He smirked and adjusted his hand on the steering wheel. "Oh yeah? Like what?"

I smiled deviously. "You don't remember?"

"Nope. That day is a total blur in my mind. What did I say?"

I opened my mouth to speak but then shut it again. "Just some dumb things. You thought I was your Mom for like an hour. And you kept asking me weird stuff like why are we underwater and how I got Steve Carrel to come see you."

"Oh God, that's rich. You take any videos?"

"Nah, I felt bad for you." I said. I looked back outside the window. I didn't want to make things awkward so I changed the subject before he could ask any more questions.

"God, it's so nice today."

"Yeah. Too nice to be cooped up in a windowless box all day." I nodded and shimmed deeper into my seat, feeling the warmth drag me deeper into the plush. I was in love with the heated seats even if it's not the right season to use them.

"Too nice for school." Carter challenged again, wiggling his eyebrows at me excitedly. I rolled my head around to look at him from my slouched position in the passenger's seat.

"Are you thinking of skipping? Today?"

Carter nodded enthusiastically. "Well this is a first for you. I thought you wanted to be better for your Mom?" He smacked his lips and stopped at a light.

"Skipping school is not selling drugs, ok? Besides, I figured it's time to let me be the bad kid for once."

"Hey, I'm not a bad kid. I left a cute sticky note on my Dad's car this morning."

"Oh, good for you. Did it say something like, you're making dinner tonight. I am never doing anything for you picky assholes again."

"No, actually, that was last week. This one was something about how he should stop leaving the empty carton of milk in the fridge because it really bums me out when I've already poured my cereal in a bowl."

"Yes, there it is. Such a great daughter."
I rolled my eyes.

"So, how about it?"

"What about your mountain of make-up work?"

"I'm gonna have to do it all sometime. It can wait another day. Besides, I heard that there's a *hot* waitress that works at this diner called O'Malley's. Maybe she's working today." Carter teased, emphasizing the word hot just to make me uncomfortable. I wrinkled my nose and made a noise of debate.

"Pleaseeeeeeeeeeeeeeee." he begged, drawing out the word until he had to take a breath of air.

"We skip at least once a week. I already have a test to make up in Chemistry that I missed when we skipped last Tuesday."
Carter made a strange noise in the back of his throat to annoy me.
I shook my head. "Ok, fine, I give up. It's too nice to care anyways."

"Yeah!" Carter whooped and changed lanes to make a U-turn. We pulled into the parking lot of O'Malley's at around 8:30. Carter held open the door for me as we entered and I curtsied.

I waved as I recognized Sawyer's face serving a table across the room and I took a seat in a booth in the corner.

"Hey darling!" Sawyer smiled at me as she approached our table, grabbing two menus from underneath the podium up front.

"Hey Sawyer." I replied in between a soft laugh. Carter raised his eyebrows at me. as she laid the menus down in front of each of us.

"Shouldn't you be in school right now?"
Sawyer hugged me and stroked my hair.

"We should not be in school actually because there was a devastating fire that burned down the gym and we are not allowed back for the next few days."

Sawyer laughed wildly. "Does that mean you can cover my shift for me tomorrow?"

"No, sorry I have school." I replied with a guilty smile.

"And is this that boy Carter you told me about?" she questioned, gesturing to him lazily with her hand.

Carter grinned up at her. "That must be me."

"Well hello, I'm Sawyer. Good to finally meet you."

"You too." He said, shaking her hand limply.

Carter was never the most vocal with strangers. I think that's something about him that I always liked. Seeing him act so shy around people he didn't know.

"Well anyways, I'm sure you kids are hungry so let's start with something to drink."

We each ordered a pile of pancakes and drowned them in pecan flavored syrup. I cheekily asked Sawyer for an extra plate and she rolled her eyes.

We took turns sipping on our huge glasses of milk and glancing outside at the warm May landscapes.

"So," Carter started, sucking down the last of the drink. "What do you want to do today? See a movie?"

"Nah, I'm strapped for cash. Putting my paychecks into savings nowadays."

"Really? That's unlike you."

"I barely even spend that much cash."

"You go out to eat almost once a day."

"Yeah. With you. To Taco Bell."

"Fair enough." He leaned back in his seat and blew air out of his lips. "Ok so some place cheap, preferably free. Um, my house."

"Your mom's home."

"Your house?"

"Sam."

"Shit."

I looked outside again at the blue skies and dirty windows, smiling and hugging my jacket closer to my body.

"What about the docks?"

"The docks? It's Monday, it's gonna be crowded with retirees.

"Exactly. It'll be fun."

"Hmm."

"Just come on."

"Fine." We paid for our pancakes and milk, each of us giving Sawyer a small tip and a long love note on the receipt.

--

We pulled up to the docks just before 11, pulling the Camry into the crowded parking lot.

We walked down the long pier and down towards where the boats were docked. The dock itself was too crowded with people for us to jump the fence so we settled onto a bench with our to-go cups of water from O'Malley's and a pack of jolly ranchers.

"God I could really go for a crunch wrap supreme right now," Carter suggested as I laid down on the bench, popping a jolly rancher into my mouth.

"Seriously? You are unbelievable."

He laughed and moved my feet, just both of us alone together on the pier.

That afternoon was slow and easy, something I'd craved for a long time but never expected to show. Sitting cross-legged on a bench by the water for hours, just talking.

I looked out into the white caps and breathed deeply as Carter sprung off the bench, running out towards the edge of the road that was parallel to the marina. I let the laziness of the afternoon pour into me, staring off at Carter's retreating body and the waves way off on the horizon. I sat there like that for a long time, just enjoying the silence and letting my eyes rest.

"I don't understand why you do that yourself." I glanced up at Carter as he approached with a frown on face. I looked around me confusedly.

"Do what? Enjoy myself?"

He shook his head and sat down next to me, spreading his legs widely into my space.

"Do you mind?" I asked, slightly offended by his previous remark.

"You just sit there alone. With your thoughts racing around everywhere. It's not good for you- dark thoughts start to come up." I rolled my eyes.

"Maybe for you, sunshine, but some of us are not completely dependent on other people to be content."
He put his hands up defensively.

"Hey, I'm just saying. Maybe instead of sitting here thinking, you could run over to the edge of the water with me as we pretend to push each other in."
I sighed and shook my head. "Don't try to be cute."
We were quiet. He knew he was right and I knew it too, but I would never admit that.
Carter perked up suddenly and started digging around in his backpack.

"Hey, I almost forgot," he pulled out something wrapped in a brown paper bag and handed it to me. "I got you something."
I looked at him suspiciously. "What? Why?"

"I just wanted to."
I opened up the creased bag and peeked inside. Inside of it was a purple hat. It was a good-looking hat in my favorite shade of purple, a deep color that reminded me of violet flowers or that one good flavor of Gatorade. The letters DC were displayed on the front in dark, black thread.

"District of Columbia?" I asked amusedly as I turned the hat around, adjusting the strap in the back.

"No. Well, that's probably what it's *supposed* to stand for but not in our case. It's Dylan and Carter, get it? I saw it at some touristy place in Atlanta."

"Oh," I said as Carter smiled at me encouragingly.

I laughed at him and crumpled up the brown paper bag, pulling the hat on my head and tucking some loose strands of hair behind my ears. I never really wear hats, but this one felt right.

"Ya like it?" I asked, posing dramatically as his green eyes lingered on my face.

"You look great."

"Thanks. This has now become a quintessential part of my wardrobe." I remarked.

"It better." He said, swatting at the rim of my new hat.

"Don't think this means I'm not mad at you anymore."

13.

October 25, 2017

I waited for Martha outside of therapy for an hour before I accepted she was probably too drunk to show up. I'd have to do things the old-fashioned way and walk home, AKA, the walk of shame for kids whose parents don't care. It was a half hour walk tops. I begrudgingly stood up from the old bench by the main office entrance and walked toward home. The rain began the minute my left foot slammed onto the pavement by the street. I sighed at my luck and let the rain pour over me. Each house's display of Halloween decorations was more elaborate than the last. People took Halloween pretty seriously in this part of town.

I walked for a couple miles drowning in the rain and feeling my clothes begin to droop and stick to my skin.
A faded Jeep Cherokee pulled up next to me and rolled down the window. I looked around the neighborhood warily.

"Hey, is that you kid?"
My neighbor Ida's face peered out from the driver's seat.
I shielded my eyes from the rain and nodded vigorously, walking up slowly to the passenger side of the car.

"What are you doing, get in here!"
I pulled open the door on the passenger side and threw my backpack in the backseat.

"Thanks." I breathed as I pulled the seatbelt across my lap.

"Yeah, sure kid. What are you doing walking home in the rain? Where's Martha?"

I pulled down the hood of my rain jacket and settled into the seat. Ida's an avid smoker and, from the smell of her car, has a harder time putting a cig down than I thought.

"Too drunk to remember she has a teenage daughter probably."

Ida laughed and turned down the radio.

"Sorry I don't mean to laugh it's just, that's so Martha. Really just a responsible mother, a real catch."

She laughed some more and I stared at her incredulously. I smiled a little and felt a laugh rising in my throat.

"Yeah."

I found myself laughing with Ida at my Mom. I was really laughing too. We laughed even as Ida ran over every pothole in the street and went speeding down the road, her windshield wipers flying over the front windshield. I laid a hand on the dash and suddenly became very aware of the fact that I was in my neighbor's car. Ida's car. A car that had seen more accidents than stunt cars from Furious 5 or whatever probably.

"Can you slow down please?" I urged as Ida continued to laugh.

"I'm going the speed limit kid."

"Yeah but it's raining aren't you supposed to go slower when it's raining?"

"Nah then they'd have a sign underneath the speed limit saying how slow to go when it's raining."

"Please stop the car." I shouted.

Ida hit the brake hard and I felt the car jerk beneath us. She pulled off the road, the rain continuing to beat harshly against the window. I gripped the armrest and breathed hard, feeling my heart beat fast in my chest. I had the sudden urge to throw up and pass out at the same time.

"What-Oh my God kid, I'm sorry. I forgot. Sometimes I don't think."

Ida peered over, looking concerned.

"Hey kid, you ok? I was only going 35. We're fine, the car's stopped, ok? Hey look, my foot is off the gas pedal." She put her hands up defensively to show they were off the steering wheel.

I shook my head slowly and took my hand off the armrest, feeling like I was in a daze.

"Yeah, no, I'm fine. I don't mind walking the rest of the way," I said reaching for the door handle.

"No sweetie, don't get your backpack, put your backpack down. I'll drive slow I swear. I can't let you walk home in this tsunami." I settled back into the seat, my hands tensing up from the anxiety I still felt about driving with Ida.

She pulled her car off from the side of the road and continued driving, slower this time.

Ida pulled into my driveway after refusing to go over twenty miles per hour the whole way home. I lost count of how many times people beeped at us and how unfazed Ida was by them.

"How is it possible that *you* of all people have your driver's license and I failed the test." I asked nervously.

"I actually failed the first couple times."

"First couple?"

"Yes. Don't judge me, I drive you here for free."

"We're neighbors."

"Whatever."

Ida took the key out of the ignition.

"Thanks Ida, really."

"Sure kid."

I pulled my backpack out from the back seat and started to pull the hood of my rain jacket over my head.

"You got therapy tomorrow too?"

"Not till next Tuesday."

"Well what say I pick you up again and we do something?"

"You and me?"

"Yeah, it'll be fun. We can drive to some weird place and buy beef jerky from the grocery store."

I laughed and looked at the window of my living room, the light from the lamp by the door casting a bright shadow out into the rain.

"Yeah actually. I'd love to."

"Ok great. What time you need me to come get you?"

"Um 3:15? You can just pull around the front."

"Perfect, see you then kid."

"Awesome."

"Bye Dylan. Say hey to your Mom for me."

I ran out into the rain and up to my house, slamming the door behind me and listening to our Halloween wreath fall off the door. I pulled down the hood of my rain jacket and was greeted with the sight of my mom's face smashed into the armrest of the couch.

She raised her head slowly when she heard the door slam and her eyes widened at my disheveled body.

"Hey, I'm Dylan. Do you live here?"

"Shit."

"Oh sorry, mom. You're so drunk I thought you were somebody else."

Martha groggily picked up her head from the couch and blew air out of her mouth. "Hey, I'm not. I forgot." she stammered, slurring her speech. "Why you all wet?"

"Oh my God. That's truly pathetic. Did you see your old boyfriend on tv again?"

She didn't answer but she grumbled something under her breath. "Get over it! He's famous and you're not! You've got a family now, you're supposed to be a mother. Drinking a whole bottle of wine is not gonna change that."

I heard the door close behind me and saw my dad standing there with a briefcase and an umbrella in his hand. "Hey kiddo." he began, smiling at me while putting down his briefcase. I gestured to Martha and he shook his head.

"Hey babe." He said with a sigh.

I stared at him unamused. "Really? That's all you have to say?" He shrugged.

I shook my head. "Grow a pair, dad. Your wife is drinking herself into oblivion because of Daniel Pitts."

I ran upstairs before I could be yelled at and instantly scribbled a note to leave by my mom's dresser. Ida is picking me up.

14.

Next Tuesday

Ida pulled up in front of therapy right on time and beeped the horn twice even though I was standing right next to the car. She pushed up her red glasses on her face as I hopped in, slamming the door behind me. She wore skinny jeans with red paint splatters and a t-shirt that read, Stop Whining Drink Wine. Ironic.

"Hey kid." she said as I threw my stuff in the back seat and pulled the seatbelt across my chest.

"Hey Ida."

"How was therapy?"

"Eh."

"Yup, sounds about right."

"How's McDonald's?"

"Ugh, I can't believe those idiots sometimes. Someone came up to me today and tried to order French toast. Can you believe it? Fucking asshole. Of all the things on the menu he chooses something we don't even have."

"So what'd you do?"

"One of the cooks threw a couple of buns in a bag with some maple syrup. That'll teach her to order something stupid."

"That's what I love about you Ida. Always so crafty."

"Yeah, Randy's getting on my nerves again though. Calling me out for the dumbest things. I gotta take a break."

I gestured to her jeans.

"You been painting today?"

"Uh, yeah, I'm making this cool black arch to put on my driveway for Halloween. Cut the tree down myself, sanded it down, glossed it up, and now I'm painting it dark black and red."
I looked at her oddly. "Where did you cut down a tree?"
"My backyard."
"Are you allowed to do that?"
"It's my property, isn't it?"
"Oh God."
I sat up higher in the passenger seat and watched as we passed by several drug stores and Stop and Shops.
"Where are we even going anyways?"
"I have no idea, I usually just drive around until I see a pretty looking place and then I pull over."
"Really?"
"Yup."
"Where have you stopped before?"
"Lots of places. One time a garden nursery, a pool noodle factory, even a stepping stone museum."
I wrinkled my nose in amusement.
"Where do you find these places?"
"Oh, they're everywhere."
We passed by a particularly run-down strip mall and suddenly I had an idea.
"You ever been roller skating?"
"Roller skating? I haven't done that for probably twenty years."
"Well, I know a place that I think you might like."

--

Ida and I bought a liter of Coke from George and sat down by the rink, watching the other people spin around and around. I admired the bat decorations that were hanging from the ceiling. The DJ was playing Michael Jackson on repeat. We left our skates on as we talked and caught our breath.

"You doing anything for Halloween tomorrow?" she asked as she sipped loudly from her can. She was spread out across the bench with her glasses so low they looked like they would fall off. She kept bumping her knee against mine under the table.

"Probably not. I'm a little too old now anyway."
Ida's eyes widened behind her thick red frames. "Too old? Kid, I'm almost 70 years old and *I'm* dressing up."
I laughed. "What are you dressing up as?"

"I'm being Rachel, from friends."

"What?"

"Yeah."

"What are you gonna wear for that?"

"Well, contacts and a wedding dress basically."

"Oh. Cool." I thought for a second about the image of Ida as Rachel from friends. Hmm.

"So you're a senior now, huh?" Ida asked.

"Yeah, I guess."

"How's it feel?"

"Oh, I don't know. Turning out to be kind of disappointing so far."

"Yeah, well, disappointment comes cheap around here, that's why everyone seems to have it."

"Yeah." I said as I looked out across the roller rink. The sight of a tall middle-aged man with long brown hair caught my eye and I suddenly had a brilliant idea.

"Hey, you know what? I just thought of a great idea for a costume."

"Really? What you got kid?"

"You ever heard of the actor Daniel Pitts?"

15.

<u>November 8, 2017</u>

The best kind of mornings are the ones with sun. The ones where tilting your head back to feel the rays of light on your neck make you feel warm and loved by the world itself. When the sun dies a little with each season it makes life seem bleaker somehow. Maybe I have that seasonal depression thing. Maybe it's just everyone. There's little that cheers me in the months of winter, although I claim the cold brings out the color in my pale cheeks and I get to wear my good socks. I don't really care about all of that though.

I raise my head when I hear a monotonous beeping sound from my bedside table. A small and whiny alarm that does little to warn me of the inevitable day that waits beyond its shrill tones.

I'd rather wake up to the sound of the Smiths or something but that seems impractical, especially since it makes me want to stay in even more to sit and just listen. I slam my hand down on the snooze and wait, curling myself up in my white blankets. Cocooned in my warm bed, wishing I could lay down for just one more minute. I get up nevertheless and shuffle my feet onto the carpet, rubbing my eyes and trying to stay upright. My head swims with exhaustion despite the seven hours I managed to clock in that night. A loud knock on the door resonates throughout my small room. Martha barges in and I inwardly roll my eyes.

"What." I say sleepily.

"Good morning to you too. Just making sure you're up."

"Well, I'm up."

"Good. Get dressed. We've gotta leave in like twenty minutes."

I nod slowly as she backs out of my room.

I pull on a sweater that's too big and some skinny jeans and run downstairs. I'm instantly greeted with the smell of good coffee in my nostrils.

"Smells good. What's for breakfast?"

"Bagel," my mom says, shoving an overly toasted and under buttered half into my hand.

"Chill out, we have like twenty minutes before we have to leave."

"I know, I was hoping we could get there early so I had time to run some errands while you wait."

"Oh, great. Just wait till right before we leave to tell me."

"Sorry honey, I got a lot on my mind. Have you seen my purse?"

I rolled my eyes as she ran hurriedly around the living room. I think she's still mad at me from Halloween. I grabbed the keys from the front room and stepped into my sneakers, pulling my hat off of its hook by the door.

"Nope. I'm gonna be in the car, ok?"

No answer. I sighed and opened up the door, pulling my hat down onto my forehead. Turning slowly, I jumped at the sight of a familiar face.

A simple smile, vague and new. Not like the others I received in passing between classes. A real one with teeth and feeling. Only the ones you get from people who have lost, people who genuinely care. That smile, so familiar.

"Hey Dylan."

Carter's brother, TJ. He looked at me sadly, he seemed somehow different. I hadn't seen him since before. I barely even saw him then. When I did, he was kind. Carter was the only one who ever really trusted him I think. He tried to keep away from the family after his arrest. I'm not really sure what happened with his case, but the relationship between TJ and his mom was never the same.

"Oh my God TJ, it's so good to see you." I leaned forward and hugged him, finding it hard to mask the shock and surprise in my face. I buried my head in his shoulder, smiling deep into the folds of his ski jacket. It smelled like his house.

"It's good to see you too Dylan." he said with a small smile.

"How are you? How is your mom?" I asked.

TJ breathed deeply and shrugged. "We're doing alright."

I nodded slowly. "What are you doing here TJ?"

He looked down at his hands. He held something small and square wrapped in a brown paper bag.

"Um, I actually have something for you."

I nodded and ran my fingertips over my palm.

"Oh, ok. Well, do you wanna come in? We're just about to leave but I'm sure we can spare a few-"

"No, no. That's ok. It'll just take a second."

I smiled and nodded again. "Oh, ok."

He ducked his head and ran his thumb over the square object in his hand. Breathing deeply.

I put my hand on his shoulder. "Is everything-ok TJ?"

"Yeah, yeah. Sorry. It's just really good to see your face."

I pursed my lips and looked at the ground.

"Anyways, I've brought something for you. We were cleaning through some of his old stuff. Carter's stuff. We found lots of his old medals and comic books, and there were a bunch of those old candy wrappers shoved in his drawers. You know, those Jolly Ranchers?"

I laughed softly and nodded my head.

"Yeah, I remember. His favorites."

"Yeah. Well, I found this old notebook in there too. I thought it was for school but when I looked through it, it wasn't. I think it's his journal." He held out the square object in his hand and handed it to me. A notebook, small and black.

"Wow. This is-. I had no idea he had something like this." I swallowed the lump in my throat that was beginning to form.

"Yeah, me neither."

I carefully removed the bag from the cover and scanned the outside of the journal. Small and leather and worn.

"Why give this to me? You're his family TJ." I didn't look in his eyes. Too afraid of crying.

He nodded and looked at the ground, intertwining his fingers.

"You're his family too Dylan. And I know that if he were still here today, he'd want you to have it."

I stuck the notebook back in its bag and put it under my jacket, looking back at the door.

"Thank you, TJ." We hugged and separated again. Our eyes both saying what we couldn't.

I heard the door slam and I turned around.

"Fucking Paul stealing my purse all the goddamn time." She turned on her heel and we both stared.

"Why aren't you in-oh. TJ. What are you doing here?"

I hugged my jacket closer to my chest as Martha's eyes narrowed slightly.

"He's just saying hey, mom."

TJ nodded. "How are you, Mrs. Anderson?"

"I'm doing well TJ, how about yourself?" she replied descending the front steps of the house.

"Doing just fine."

"Glad to hear it."

TJ nodded and backed up slightly.

"Well, I'll let you two go then. Mom's probably wondering where I am. Good talking to you two."

We both nodded and watched him go.

"Bye TJ." I called after him.

"Bye Dyl."

"Bye.' I called again. I watched as he made his way down the driveway. I felt the outline of the notebook in my jacket and bit my lip, the confrontation I had with Brady weeks ago crawling its way into my mind.

"Hey TJ." I shouted, running down the driveway. The cold wind blew harshly into my face and made my eyes water. I slowed to a stop at the end of the driveway, TJ waiting for me to say something. "Before you go, do you know a guy named Brady Dean?"

TJ stared at me for a few seconds and blinked. "You mean the guy that used to bully you?"

"Uh, yeah."

He hesitated. "Just from you and Carter. Why?"

Martha's voice cut in from behind me. "Honey, let's go!" she yelled.

I stepped back from the edge of the driveway again. "Just wondering."

I watched as TJ made his way to his car. "Come by the house sometime Dyl, it's weird not seeing you there."

I nodded as he got into his car and I waved. I walked back up the driveway. Mom and I got in the car and turned on the heat, letting the car warm up.

"That was nice of him to stop by like that. Just as spontaneous as his brother huh."

"Yeah, it was cool."

"What did you guys talk about?" I could tell she wanted to say more. To tell me to stay away from TJ.

"Just saying hi." I felt the lining of the notebook by my hip again and smiled as we pulled out of the driveway. TJ was still sitting in his car as we drove away.

--

I kept the notebook in my jacket until we got home. I ran upstairs and locked the door to my room, carefully pulling the notebook out of its place. It was warm.

The notebook. Thick and worn, the cover leather and bound with a thick strip of twine. I carefully unraveled the journal, picking through the multitude of pages, silent and numb. The pages were sloppy and full, spidery handwriting with dotless i's ran rampant across the spaces. A few foreign entities were shoved into the spine of the book, pages ripped and folded as if cared for by some careless soldier. I knew that it wasn't that way. The owner, a caring boy with eternal eyes and the worst handwriting you've ever seen. It really was illegible.

I struggled to decode the messages he had written, I wanted to read the whole thing over one night. I didn't absorb the words then, I just wanted to read it. To understand why he cared so much. It was…hard. It took me hours to read the first three pages, I read each word twenty times to make sure it was right. The first page had a date-February 20, 2009. He was nine. It was weird, reading his words from when he was still young, when he could still run through the trees all morning without collapsing. I'd forgotten how much I missed that kid. I sat for hours, typing his journal onto my laptop so I could read it again and again. It's simple, yet I felt completely different sitting in my chair than I had when I sat down.

My mom told me to start writing down my thoughts so I won't talk so much. She thought I wouldn't do it, but I am. That's right mom, bet you're surprised! It's what I do.

Today is Friday, I went to school sort of but I left early. Mom and I went to the doctors and he gave me some candy and a dumb note that I already lost. Then I went home and saw Liam, my best friend. We went and ran in the woods until dinner, some sort of gross meat again. I found a rock in the woods. It's cool.

It was stupid. Half of it didn't even make sense.

I read it twice and cried.

--

I stayed up all night thinking, not being able to sleep. I wanted so badly to read more but I wanted to savor what he had written. After I read the journal, I'll never be able to hear new words from him ever again. I thought about that for a while and the fog rolled in. It always comes when I think I've finally found peace. A thick fog that rolls in through me, settling deep inside my stomach. It's a cruel thing. It turns my memories inside out. All Carter. All gone. It's taunting and debilitating. I feel nauseous and resentful. I feel angry and not real. I go limp to contain the magnitude of this emotional pain, crawling inside my bed for the weekend, wondering why I'd ever want to get up at all. I die for a while, but get back up again so I don't miss too much. She's better than me, he doesn't care about me, this doesn't matter, those sorts of things. The fog rolling in again to consume me forever, an endless maze of depression.

16.
<u>November 9, 2017</u>

At some point, my brain finally shut up and let me crash on the floor. I woke up to a small hand shaking my shoulder. I groggily opened up my eyes and yawned. Martha stood above me with a concerned expression on her face. "Mom? What time is it?"

She scowled and sat on my bed. "Almost 12. Are you feeling ok?"

I smiled and nodded, stretching. "Yeah, why? What's up? You're still not used to my afternoon snoozes?"

She laughed softly and shook her head.

"I'm just wondering. What's that you're reading?" she questioned, reaching for the journal that was tucked between my arms. I grabbed it back from her hands and shut it hastily.

"Nothing, just an old journal." She eyed the book cautiously.

"Is it porn?"

"What? No! Get out!"

"Honey, you don't have to be embarrassed if it is. It's human nature."

"It's not porn, gosh. It's just personal."

"Ok, whatever you say. I'm going to the grocery store. You need anything?"

"No. Is Sam here?"

"No, he's at work."

"Ok, ok."

"You need something?"

"No."

I waited until she left and ate a toaster strudel, then I grabbed my bike and rode down to see Rosie.

--

My eyes lingered on Carter's board as I walked briskly through the front door, the journal clasped tightly in my left hand. The light from the disco ball made the room spin around me.

I took a second to look out at the rink, scanning the room for any sign of Rosie or George.

Nowhere.

I sat down on a bench beside the snack bar and looked down again at the journal. I considered barging into Rosie's office but I stopped myself.

I looked up again at the rink and furrowed my brow. I felt like I had something urgent to tell someone and yet I didn't have anything to say. I was hit with the realization that I came storming in here with absolutely no purpose.

Why did I come here? What do I have to say?

Nothing. Nothing at all.

I wrapped the journal's twine tighter around the cover and I stood up, holding it close to my chest. I didn't come here to talk to Rosie, I came here to talk to Carter. To tell him that I found his journal because that's what I've always done. Talked to him about nothing.

Well, I can't really do that anymore.

It's hard to let go when it's all you know.

17.
Before

Saturday morning, I had the tv on old reruns of the Twilight Zone. The blanket draped over my bare legs made me sweaty but I liked that cozy little reminder of soft linen. I sank lower in the dusty leather couch and stretched my legs over the armrest. I could and often had been spending entire weekends like this.

The week, when I got the letter, I already had expected a no. My mom on the other hand, did not.

"We just have to figure out what you're doing wrong. Maybe you should retake math again, you know you only got a B."

"No mom, math is fine. It's almost summer anyways. It's a little late."

"What if you reapply at your old job, huh? That's something! Colleges love to see that type of stuff."

"No mom you know I can't go back right now I-"

"Ok well you gotta help me out honey, I mean I feel like I'm dragging you through this whole thing! *You're* the one who's actually going to be going to these colleges so maybe you should stop moping around and actually do something."

I flipped around on the couch, feeling that agitated angry feeling rise within me.

"Ok, Martha. I get up every day at 6. I go to school for ten plus hours. I'm taking multiple college courses, I tutor people in history. And then, because *you're* too drunk from a long day of doing nothing, I gotta make dinner too."

"Every kid that goes to the colleges you're applying to does those same things, Dylan. You can't expect that to be enough. And stop calling me Martha, you know I hate that."
I scoffed and sunk back onto the couch. "You're such a hypocrite." Martha grabbed the remote out of my hand.

"Don't talk to me like that. I'm your mother, I'm only trying to help you." She yelled.

"Ok well stop helping! You're making me apply to these ivy league schools that I will *never* get into! Do you really think they're generous enough to let an average student like me get into their school? Let alone give me a dime to help pay for it! They're not gonna do it. They're just not! I'm not Sam, mom for the last time. Ok? I'm not. I'm Dylan, hi! How you doing? Don't think we've met before. Get that through your head because if you don't, I think I'm gonna lose my mind."

"Dylan I-," Martha sat down next to me on the couch, trying her best to level her shaky voice. "I never mean to compare you to Sam, you know that. I'm sorry it's-it's unfair to you I know.

"I would love to hear a halfhearted apology some other day mom, but right now I've gotta go." I said as I jumped off the couch, the blanket falling off my legs onto the floor.

"No, honey-where are you going? I'm about to make dinner, why don't you stay."

"Really? Dinner. That's new. But I can't, I promised Carter we'd hang out today. I'll be back later tonight."

"Well alright, but where are you going anyways?"

"Just driving around and seeing things, like we always do."
I grabbed my hat off the kitchen table and walked out of the door. The pale Camry sat waiting for me in front of the driveway.

Carter listened to me as I ranted about my mom and we drove into downtown Alliance. It was a small downtown area, but there was one building tall enough to be considered a high rise. It was still being built but people were saying it was gonna be a bank. It ended up just being more apartments. We parked the car behind it and snuck in through the back, making our way up to the top from the staircase. We sat atop the tall building, looking down at the drunk people by the supermart and all the people in the apartment complex across the street. I could see a tv playing in one of the rooms. Shark Week or something. There were two people having dinner in another. I saw a girl crying by herself in a room near the top. I think she was in her closet or something. I frowned at her.

"This is so cool," Carter said as he stared at the apartment building.
We leaned over the edge of the roof, looking down at the little ant people and guessing where they were going. "Yeah. It's pretty cool."

"I feel like I'm watching tv but every channel is someone else's life, you know? Like every little apartment window or sidewalk square is a different station."
I smiled at him. "Didn't think about it that way. But I like it."
I looked back at the poor girl crying in her closet. "Why do you think she's crying over there?"
He followed my gaze and squinted his eyes. "I don't know. Maybe she just found out her ex-boyfriend is now a famous movie star." Carter said, looking at me seriously. I smirked at him and we both started to laugh. We looked back over at the crying girl and she was staring straight at us. She closed the blinds on her window and we decided to head back down.

18.

<u>November 17, 2017</u>

"See, isn't this beautiful? My mom and I at the beach during sunset. A collection of awestruck couples surrounded us, kissing and cuddling, in the gross pornographic way.

"I hate the beach." I kicked the raw and cold sand out from under my toes and crossed my arms over my chest. The air was getting colder as Summer turned into fall and the waves sprayed its salty foam across my flannel-clad torso and stringy hair. I didn't like that.

"You don't hate the beach," my mother instructed, drawing her thin white blouse over her t-shirt and walking slowly across the beach. Her feet left small indents in the damp sand.

"Yes, I do. I tell you all the time. It's such a hassle and my skin always gets fried. It fucking sucks."

"Don't use that word, Dylan. You know I hate that. And don't be so whiny, I thought you used to come here all the time."
I grimaced and closed my eyes as the wind began to blow softly.

"Yes. *Used* to. Past tense."
We were silent for a while as we 'enjoyed' the sounds of the night. The crickets, the oohing couples, the soft waves.

"Why don't you start going more again? It's so nice here. You can invite a friend."

"I'm here with you right now, aren't I?"

"You know what I mean, someone your age."

"It wouldn't feel right."

"Why, because of him?"

"No, because I don't like the beach."

"Honey," she sighed and paused. "We both know this isn't about you not liking the beach. I know it's been a couple months since he-well-passed away-but that doesn't mean you should hold on like you're doing. It's not good for you to just sit around by yourself all day."

I pursed my lips and stayed quiet, hoping the sound of the seagulls and crashing waves would drown her out.

"I- I just want you to know that despite how you may feel, life is not over for you. He'd want you to move on sweetie. He'd want you to get out-"

"Carter."

"Yes."

"You can say his name you know. It's not a bad word."

"I know sweetie I just wasn't sure how you'd react if I said it."

"How I'd react if you mentioned the name of my best friend? It's normal, mom. It doesn't have to be weird."

We kicked sand and didn't talk a little more.

"Did you bring me out here to tell me that?"

She shrugged and moved closer to me.

"Not the whole reason. You just seemed so cooped up in that house, I thought it'd be a good idea for the both of us to get some fresh air."

I nodded and bit my lip.

"Yeah."

We walked till we reached the docks at the east end of the beach and watched as the last trickles of the sun fizzled out below the horizon.

"We should head back. It's almost eight, your dad might worry."

I held my gaze with the rays of gold between the orange backdrop and sighed.

"Yeah, ok."

We turned around and headed back down the beach.

"Why don't you talk to me?"

I looked at her weird. "We're talking right now."

"You know what I mean. This is not talking."

"Fine. You want me to be honest with you?"

"Yes. Please."

"Ok. But only because I know dad doesn't have the guts to say anything," I said as I looked down at my hands. I had the realization that this would be the first time I had a real talk with her sober self. "You are an alcoholic. I know you keep saying that wine doesn't count," I said using air quotes, "but in your case, it does. You drink yourself to sleep practically every night probably because you've spent the last twenty years of your life wishing you had married your old boyfriend Daniel Pitts instead of dad." My mom opened her mouth to speak but I continued. "You know it and I know it and dad knows it."

"Honey that's not-"

"Please. Just let me finish talking and you can say whatever you want. I know you love dad. He tells me stories sometimes of when you two were dating. But you act like we're all a huge burden on you. And it pisses me off that you spend all your time feeling sorry for yourself that you never give me any time to talk to you about my own problems. You're my mother. And the only reason you're not happy now is you think that you chose wrong. But you didn't. You have a family. And that's more than Daniel Pitts can say for himself." I looked down at our feet and back up at my Mom's face. She had a look like she was waiting for me to keep talking so she could slap me.

"Honey I am not obsessed with Daniel Pitts. And I'm not an alcoholic either. But I appreciate the advice." Martha spat. I looked at her with a frown.

"Fine. Don't listen. You know it's true."

"Well, I don't know about that but thanks."

"You wanted me to be honest."

"We don't have to talk anymore."

"Fine, works for me."

That never lasts. If I held my breath until she started talking again, I wonder if I would have enough time to pass out.

"Sam got another scholarship for school."

"Oh, good for him." That wasn't long enough.

"You gonna start applying to some soon?"

"I told you mom I already did."

"Well, apply to some more."

"I've got a lot going on right now but I will do them when I get a chance."

"Sounds to me like you don't really care."

"Didn't we just talk about this last week? I told you I'm doing everything I can."

"Well I don't think you are. We don't have the money to send you to those colleges Dylan, you have to work harder to-"

"I am working hard! I've been working hard every day for the past four *months*. I'm using every ounce of what I have in me to just get out of bed. I don't have much left in me after all the bullying and the bitching and the antagonizing. I do shit for everybody and I don't get so much as a nod of thanks."

"Stop that-"

"Oh, of *course* this is happening right now."

"What are you talking about nothing is happening." Martha looked around us

"We're arguing. You said you brought me out here to relax, to get out of the house. But everywhere we go, we argue. You lecture me, you get mad, it's always something with you."

"That's because you can't see that you're destroying your life right now Dylan. You're young, you should be out there having fun."

"Let's just not talk anymore, ok?"

My mom shook her head as we approached our station number.

"Time doesn't stop Dyl, you have to keep going."

"I want it to stop."

"But you can't. So you have to stop worrying about it."

"I want it to stop."

"Stop saying that."

"Just stop."

She hugged me for the first time in 7 months.

--

Martha and I pulled into the driveway just before nine. I went upstairs and laid down on my bed, just thinking. That's never really been good for me though. I looked at Carter's journal on my desk and ambled toward it. It was weird staring at the journal, wondering whether I wanted to read every word all at once or throw it into the fireplace. I figured I may as well read it since it's here, you know?

I locked my door quietly and laid down on the floor on my stomach.

May 5th, 2017

Brady and a bunch of those other guys caught me in the courtyard in between class again today. They pushed me around and kept saying shit to me. I wanted to swing at them so bad but I can't disappoint my mom after TJ's arrest.

A lot of the last ten entries I read had something to do with Brady. I guess this is his way of getting it all off his chest.

So I just took it and tried to walk away. Brady pushed me down on the ground and I was so fucking angry, I almost did it. But Dylan saved me.

I smiled at the mention of my name, remembering how it sounded on his lips.

She must've been cutting class and saw us. I didn't ask, didn't want to pry and upset her or something.

I remember that day. I wasn't skipping, I left class to go to the bathroom and just stumbled across him. I left my book bag in class and had to make up some bullshit excuse about an emergency the next day.

We left before we got in any real trouble, getting in the Camry and going to the docks for a while. It was nice. I got home and overheard TJ talking about some lighthouse somewhere further up north. It sounded cool, maybe Dyl and I can go there on our next adventure.

I let my eyes linger on the page, re-reading the words and counting the letters in my mind. I ran my finger over the sentence with the lighthouse, thinking about the time he told me that he wanted to go there one day. He never got to go.

19.

Before

I hated being in school. That's why I skipped so much. It wasn't so much school itself. It was all due to this one class.

I approached Mr. Fitz after class with my paper. A big red D covered up half of the page of my final project. No comments, just one letter. He did that on a lot of my papers. My essay on The Grapes of Wrath, my argument writing on teachers with guns, even my introduction writing to the class about my own life. It's bullshit, English is my best, and only, good subject. It's one of the only tolerable high school classes.

The 23 other bored and sweatpants-clad crowd ran out of class as quickly as they could. Summer was in two days and we were all getting antsy.

"Hi, Mr. Fitz? Can I ask you a question real quick?" I stammered. I had been reluctant to approach him all year. I only ever did once at the beginning of the semester. It was not a pleasant conversation.
Mr. Fitz lifted his eyes off his computer and leaned back in his chair.

"Oh yes, what is it, Miss. Anderson?" I hate when teachers call you stuff like that.

"Hey, yeah it's just about my paper. All my papers actually." I pulled the delicate four-page packet off my collection of science textbooks and laid it gingerly on his desk. He pulled it towards himself with two fingers and reluctantly flipped through.

"It's just- I love English. I've always done really well in it. And I feel like I'm a pretty good writer too but all year I've gotten C's and D's and I don't know why."

He nodded and skimmed the essay, flipping back and forth between pages.

"I was just hoping you could help me out and tell me what I'm doing wrong."

He lifted his head and nodded, his face blank.

"Yeah, I'll tell you what you're doing wrong. You're overthinking the prompts, you're making it too hard. It was supposed to be a pretty standard book review but you made it..." he gestured wildly with his hands and handed the report back to me. "Complicated and wordy. Does that make sense?"

"I mean, I know that I added some extra details and stuff but I addressed the prompt like you wanted. I just like to add a little-"

"Listen, Anderson, if you'd have come to me sooner, I could've helped you with this. But you didn't and you made a bad grade. I'm sorry, that's on you. Have a great summer." I looked down at the paper in my hands and bit the inside of my cheek nervously.

"But I did exactly what you told us to do, I just went a little deeper with it."

"And did I tell you to go deeper? No, I didn't. I don't know how your other English classes operated Miss. Anderson but I'm not gonna give you a free A. Your essays are not that impressive, the extra things you're adding make everything sound childish. I'm sorry, but I've got some papers to grade."

I stood at the front of his desk for a moment, biting my lip and feeling that familiar angry feeling rise up into my chest.

"Grading some papers? Summer is in two days what could you possibly be working on?"

"Miss. Anderson, I understand that you're upset but coming to ask a question about your grades *after* you submit your final project is not very wise. Don't get angry at me for your mistake."

I pursed my lips and cleared my throat. I walked stiffly out of the room. Turning on my heel as I reached the doorway, I looked back at Mr. Fitz, relishing the feeling of never having to see him again.

"You're right Mr. Fitz. My mistake. My mistake for thinking for a second that you were even a little bit competent to understand how to properly grade papers. You're an asshole. Have a good summer." I stormed out of the school with my paper in my hand, stomping my way into the parking lot towards Carter's car.

I slammed the door to the Toyota exasperated and threw my book bag in the back seat, sinking low into the passenger seat and groaning. Isn't this just fantastic.

A knock on my window made me jump.

"Looks like you had a good day." Carter said as he opened the driver's door and climbed inside. I glared back and crossed my arms. He shut the door and adjusted his jacket, frowning at my slumped form.

"What happened?"

"Mr. Fitz is what happened. He gave me a D on my final paper. A D!" I said exasperatedly.

"AP English guy? Why'd he do that? That's your thing."

"Exactly, that's why I'm pissed."

"Let's go do shit to his car, that'll make you feel better."

I rolled my eyes and smiled.

"You always say stuff like that."

"Hey, it works."

"Nah, I'm not in the criminal mood. Besides, I called him an asshole before I left. I think that's enough vengeance for me." I sighed and watched as he turned the key in the ignition.

"You said that to a teacher? God you're crazy. And that's why I love you." I laughed as he fiddled with the radio.

"You going to work today?" he asked me.

"Nope. I got the day off."

"Nice. Guess you'll just have to come to work with me."

"Gladly."

"You know colleges don't accept freeloaders, right?"

"Ha ha. Don't tease me, I'm mad."

"Ok, sorry."

"You still thinking about Appalachian State?"

"Yup. That's my number one."

"You think they take people with a D in AP English?"

"Hmm, I don't know. Why don't you call and ask?'

--

I sat down on the counter as Carter clocked in in the back.

"Hey George," I greeted nonchalantly as a red-haired man carrying a box full of tickets walked by.

"Hey, Dylan. You actually gonna skate today or just loiter?"

"I'm going with the latter today my friend."

"Perfect," he muttered under his breath as he disappeared into the back.

"I think George hates me." I proposed as Carter came up front with his polo on.

"Nah, he hates everybody."

"Hmm."

We scanned the 4 o'clock crowd of Rosie's Roller Rink. Same old murder looking creeps with a handful of starry-eyed high schoolers thrown in. I looked over at Carter leaning over the counter with a hand on his chin. He caught my eye and smirked.

"You checking me out Anderson?"

"You wish. Although you do look stunning in those slacks."

"I knew you had a thing for me."

I rolled my eyes and hopped off the counter as Rosie came sauntering by in her too tight black jeans.

"Carter, Dylan. Glad to see you both showed up to work today."

Carter grinned sheepishly at her and I nodded.

"With all the time you spend here Dylan you could be making a fortune."

"I already have a job, Rosie."

"Yeah. As my assistant," Carter said, swinging his legs over the counter.

"How many times have I told you not to do that," Rosie replied.

"Right. Sorry boss."

"It's a wonder I still keep you kids around. Keep working hard Carter."

"Will do, Rosie."

I punched him playfully and shook my head. "You are such an ass."

"Hey, talk to me like that again and you're fired. Now go get me a corndog from good ole Georgie over there."

I rolled my eyes. "Get back to work."

20.
<u>Nov. 21, 2017</u>

It wasn't until sophomore year when I began to question my own self-awareness. Existentialism had been a unit we'd just learned in English. It was during that time that I'd thought about all the books I've read and the movies I've seen and the even the confidence I saw in other people. These things all had something in common, something that I'd lacked and wanted so much. A deep understanding of themselves or something.

I wasn't present in my own life. I looked at life through a little glass lens that makes everything just a bit blurrier. I looked through people. I began to wonder if I'd ever have a real human connection ever. Each day felt like a dream, an illusion, a movie reel I was an extra in.

I tried so hard to change that, let me tell you. I tried getting out of my head, away from what could be, what could happen. It just doesn't work. No matter what I do. I'm afraid that I've got a sickness, that I'll never be able to shake this zombie-like state I'm always *always* in. But I can't. And I might never be able to.

I want to truly look at something and understand it and not wonder if I'm missing a big part of it. Right now, I can only look past. I wonder if other people feel the same. But I'm too afraid to ask out loud. Too afraid to expose myself as the girl holding the lens, as the one that will go nowhere because she can't even see what's standing right in front of her face.

--

"I guess you could say I've been like this before Carter. Since my freshman year of high school. I thought I would be ready but I never really prepared myself for all this." I pulled on some loose thread in my jeans and continued.

"When I was young I watched those sitcoms with my mom with those, you know, graduate students pretending to be ten years younger in high school and stuff. I watched those almost every night. They made me laugh more than my actual friends could. But seriously, what a load of crap those shows are. I mean, it's high school, why is everyone driving Corvettes and singing all the time? Why are the parents the same age as their kids? It made no sense." I jiggled my foot impatiently, feeling the eyes of Dr. Lupa stare me down.

"Anyways, the tv I sat in front of every night must have numbed me or something, made me lose feeling, I don't know, something like that. Maybe it made me a little crazy. All's I know is that it changed the way I expected high school to go. I started to believe that bullshit on the screen."

"Hey."

"Sorry."

Dr. Lupa jotted something down and nodded encouragingly.

"Go on."

"When my freshman year started I was underprepared, to say the least. I've always been a bit of a sensitive kid. Such an emotional kid. It's in the genes. But, you can't be that way in high school, at least not the one I went to." I ran my thumb over my chin, jiggling my leg faster and faster.

"After a couple of years of my sensitivity combined with teenage discard for feelings, it messed me up. Now I'm sure I wasn't the only one, but it really got to me. The anxiety, expectations, everything. Everyone blurred into this mess of psychological garbage. I can't describe that right now."

"During my sophomore year, I distanced myself from my family a little more. I was angry with them, I think. For not giving me any help with anything I was dealing with. They didn't seem to care. After I ignored them for a while, I stopped spending time with two of my best friends so I could be with Carter more. He was my rock through it all, the only person that kept me going" I sat silently as Dr. Lupa jotted some more nonsense into her journal.

"And what about junior year?"

"Junior year was the same. Look, Dr. Lupa. I don't know what's wrong with me. I don't know how this all started. I only know that Carter dying made it worse. And I don't know where the end is either. But I'm here. And that's gotta mean something."
Dr. Lupa nodded slowly as I talked and looked down at her toes.

"Dylan," she began slowly. "I'm going to do everything I can to help you. You are here and you are progressing. I see a change in you every time we talk. Things will get easier, it just takes some time."

"Yeah, I hope so."
Dr. Lupa eyed me calmly. My hat pulled down over my face, swaddled lovingly by her thin white blanket. "I have to admit I'm impressed. You know this is the first time you've shown interest in actually talking with me."

"Yeah, I know."

"Do you mind if I ask what changed? Why now?"
I stayed quiet for a while, pulling again at the thread on my jeans.

"A journal was given to me a couple of days ago. Carter's journal. I didn't even know he had one. I've been reading it. Slowly. It made me realize that I'm in a lot of pain. I've just got a lot that I'm carrying around with me and I want to talk about, get rid of some of it."

"Well, that's a very good strategy." I nodded as she jotted a few more things down in her notes. "I know that this recovery process is difficult. It's not just about talking through it all. It's about picking up the pieces of yourself that you've lost by finding peace with what happened."

"Finding peace. You always say that. But how?"

"Well, what a lot of people have found to work for them is finding closure. Instead of letting the pain subside gradually, they attempt to find a way to hasten the healing process themselves."

"How can I do that?"

Dr. Lupa shrugged. "I don't know. Only you can know that."

21.
November 29, 2017

I looked out my window of the kitchen the next morning, wiping the dusty glass with the palm of my hand. Ida was inside her kitchen washing a dish in the sink or something. I went to the freezer and pushed past the leftovers from our Cracker Barrel sponsored Thanksgiving. That was the most intense hour of turkey eating ever; my family is the worst at holidays. I grabbed the waffles out of the back and set them on the counter. I saw Ida waving at me from the corner of my eye and I waved back, approaching the window and unlatching it. She smiled and did the same.

"Good Morning Ida." I sang, leaning out into the open air, pushing myself up with my toes.

"Morning kid, how'd you sleep?" I tried not to laugh at Ida's disheveled appearance. Her grey hair was splayed wildly, and her glasses were fogged up from the steam rising from the sink.

"Eh. Average."

"Me too, couldn't get the damn cricket outside of the tree by my bed to stay quiet. All it does is yap."

I laughed and leaned further into the sink.

"You eat breakfast yet kid?"

"Not yet. Thinking about making myself a homemade Eggo."

"Eggo? Oh. Eggo my ass, come on over. I'm making French toast."

I laughed and eyed her kitchen with interest. "Really?"

"Yes kid, get over here."

I didn't even bother putting on shoes as I walked the short distance between my house and Ida's. I wondered if it would be weird to knock or if I should just walk in. I pushed open the door and stepped into her house. It occurred to me as I walked in that I hadn't been in her house since I was a little kid. I wasn't sure what to expect because I hadn't remembered anything about it. The first thing that stood out to me was how warm it was in her house.

When I walked in my bare toes were met with a dusty old deep red carpet with swirly patterns on it. The smell of strong coffee and syrup stained the atmosphere and the long purple drapes by the windows reminded me of sheer seaweed. There were lots of paintings and other art pieces covering the walls, old and new. Mostly impressionist stuff that I didn't really understand. I walked through it all towards that strong smell. Ida stood in front of the stove flipping pieces of thick white bread on a greasy pan, a small stack already accumulating next to her. Her coffee pot was brewing fresh coffee by the sink.

"There she is. Have a seat anywhere kid. You want some coffee?"

"No, I'm good, I've never really liked the taste. Just the smell." I looked down at the square table. There were four chairs set around it and two plates in front of two of the chairs. I chose the one closest to the sink and sat down, pulling the chair close into the table.

"No kidding. You sound just like my sister." Ida placed a piece of french toast on the stack and placed another piece of white bread into the pan, the bread sizzling with the contact of the hot stove. She reached into the cabinet and pulled out two mugs, filling them both to the brim with the hot coffee liquid. "Just have a little bit," she teased as she set the cup next to me.

"Mine's good." I nodded amusedly and set the mug at the edge of the placemat.

"Thanks for having me over Ida."

"Anytime kiddo."

Ida flipped the pan some more and finally plopped the final piece of toast on top.

"What would you like to drink? I've got water, milk, orange juice, um, well that's about it I guess."

"Orange juice sounds great."

Ida reached into the fridge and pulled out a round jar of the orange liquid, pouring it out into a smaller glass jar with small, blue fish painted on the sides.

She laid a bottle of thick North Carolina syrup and the tall stack of french toast on the table in front of me, taking a seat to the right of me at the head of the table.

We looked at each other and she laughed.

"Well, let's dig in then."

She dug her fork into the top of the stack and pulled some slices of French toast onto her plate, I copied her movements and grabbed the bottle of syrup. I dumped too much on like I always did.

Taking a bite, I closed my eyes.

"This is amazing," I said.

"Thanks kid. Better than some frozen Eggo breakfast, right?" I nodded as I speared another piece on my plate. "You know I haven't had someone over like this in a long time."

I swallowed a big bite of syrupy goodness and wiped my mouth with my napkin. "Oh. Why not?"

"Just haven't had the time I guess." I lifted my head and saw Ida frown, just for a second. I frowned back at her and was quiet. I took a small sip of her orange juice and looked out the window at her backyard.

"It's nice." She smiled at me in a new way, almost like she was shy about having to say it. I smiled that smile back.

I raised my glass towards her.

"Well then, I'd like to make a toast."

"Whatcha got for me kid?"

I searched her face.

"To...good friends. And even better french toast."

Ida laughed and we clinked our glasses together messily. I hadn't really thought about it before, Ida being lonely in her house. I always thought her big, red glasses self was enough to keep her company. But maybe it wasn't.

"Cheers."

22.
December 3, 2017

I closed my eyes and felt the wind blow my hair back across my shoulders as I let the bike steer me towards the end of whatever road I was riding down. I had my coat zipped up to my chin and was breathing hot air down my collar.

The day was sunny but with a cold chill, like the rest of the month. I pedaled down towards this cafe called Oja's. It's a small and thin building with barely enough room to hold three booths and two tables. I walked in and ordered a small black coffee with two sugars and sat down. I think Ida's coffee addiction was rubbing off on me.

I spent some time huddled in my jacket watching people laugh while I sat alone and picked at the seam of my hoodie, trying to make sense of my reality. Today was a good day. But what makes days like today any different than days like two days before? Nothing has changed. Just the way I feel.

I looked around the coffee shop at all the people. A woman and a small child sat on the booth across from me, sharing a cup of something hot and a slice of vanilla cake. They were smiling so I smiled. Some things are just contagious like that. I looked back at the empty chair across from me and wondered who I was waiting for. Who I wanted to share a hot cup of something with.

A loud bang resounded right by my ear as a small and scared looking woman crashed into the window beside me. She pointed down the street at a man running away from her in a dark colored hoodie and skinny jeans. He had a purple purse in his hand. Now, I know it's the 21st century and all, but there is no way that's his.

I didn't have much time to think but it wasn't a hard decision. I've been so bored and alone and no one knows I'm waiting for them at this booth. Let's go do something.

I pushed myself up from the booth and ran out the door. I saw the woman who was still wildly pointing in the man's direction and I took off running.

I ran out in the street as fast as my converse clad shoes could run. Not very fast. Cardio is not my thing. Still, I'm a gangly teenager with a biking fetish and the perp in question looked like a bit of a heftier man in skinny jeans. I ran after him for two or three blocks, dodging onlookers and know-nothings on foot traffic. My breath came out in short bursts and swirled around my face in a thick fog. I saw him swing right on Leland Street down towards the docks. I picked up the pace as the area became more familiar. People watched as we ran but no one stopped us, the bystander effect or whatever I guess.

I half expected the guy to give up running as I chased him but he kept going like his life depended on it. I could feel us both slowing down as we ran downhill towards the water.

I had never appreciated the simple feeling of a glass of cold water in my hand until I ran like that. Even in the winter. I wasn't thinking about the fact that I was running towards a criminal that probably had a gun or something. I wasn't thinking about the fact that I was more running from myself than towards a guy who stole a purse.

I was thinking about how good it felt to be going somewhere with a purpose. And so I smiled. Even though the wind started running down my throat and making it feel like sandpaper, I kept on smiling. I'm apparently that crazy. I could feel my legs numbing and my heart turning. The uncontrollable beating of my heart and the sharp wheeze in my lungs. The blood ran into my throat and stuck to every pore- sweaty and numb. Numb all over yet more alive than I'd been in over four months.

I don't get out much and this guy clearly has more experience than I imagined. He slowed a bit as we approached the gate in front of the pier. He threw the bag over and hopped the fence with little difficulty. I did the same, only much less graceful, nearly slamming my face down onto the pavement in the process. We kept running as the ground beneath changed from asphalt to wood, running to the edge of the dock.

Suddenly, the guy leapt off the dock onto a small pontoon boat with an equally hefty and sketchily clad man waiting. They muttered things to each other as they frantically started the engine and pulled away from the docks. They drove off towards the water, each flipping me the bird as they went. Lovely.

I was so close.

"Damn it." I fumed to myself as I slowed to a stop by the now empty docking station.

I ran for what felt like so long- I wasn't even sure if I was moving at all by the end of it. I put my hands on my head and watched them drive away, pursing my lips and trying to slow my breathing.

The guy chose a particularly run-down section of the docks to escape from- the ones you recognize from those fishy horror films. I looked sideways down towards the other end of the dock and a wrinkled and sunburnt man with no shirt nodded at me, averting his eyes from my disheveled frame. I sat down on shaky knees between a tackle box and a yacht. The water swayed and bobbed with me as I gasped for breath. I laid my head back and closed my eyes. And I laughed.

And then he appeared.

"What the fuck." he began exasperated, his shirt dripping in sweat.

"Did you see that? I almost-I almost had him." I managed to choke out.

"You shouldn't have chased after him like that. He could have- could have had a gun or something. You could have gotten hurt."

I wiped my forehead on my t-shirt and sighed. "I'm too tired for this Carter."

Carter sputtered and sighed. "Don't do this to me right now, Dylan. Don't do this. Stop being so fucking self-destructive. Stop running from everybody. It's not gonna solve a thing." I laid my hand on the tackle box and pushed myself up with my knees.

"Jesus I was trying to help some lady out Carter, not kill the guy."

"No. You didn't chase that guy down to help anyone out but yourself. You did it because you wanted attention."

"Maybe I did want attention. And you know what? It felt good."

"Well, I'm glad you had fun because that little stunt got us nowhere."

I paced slowly and watched him warily as he sat down on the tackle box.

"Tell me how I get people to notice me. Tell me what to do because I'm almost out of ideas. I'm floundering, Carter. It's not hard to tell."

"You're right, it's not."

I frowned slightly and shook my head.

"I don't want to deal with this." I whispered to myself.

"With what?"

"What?"

"You don't want to deal with what?"

I pursed my lips.

"You said, you said you don't want to deal with *this*. You know what that means? You're acknowledging that this is real. Me, talking to your right now. You can't run from reality, Dylan. It's *always* going to catch up to you."

I chuckled. "It's not all about you Carter. Things have always been like this. You just made it worse."

"It's all about me, Dyl. Why else would I be here?"

Silence.

"Look. I'm trying to help you *move on* Dylan. Can you please just acknowledge that?"

"Oh, here comes Mr. Reality coming to bring me back to the present. Well, I for one really hate the present at the moment. Especially since I spend half my time talking to a ghost." I lamented, gesturing to him. "This is not closure. This is torture."

"I hate you. I hate what you've become."

"You hate that I still get to grow up and you can't."

"No. I hate you."

"You hate me? Carter, my best friend, hates me. Carter would never say that."

"I'm saying that right now."

"You're not Carter. You're me. I'm talking to myself."
I blinked at the Carter I was imagining and sat down in front of him, laying my head in my hands and wanting to scream in frustration. I banged my forehead against the palms of my hands, trying to keep the tears from falling down my face.

"Why am I this way? I want to live, I want to *live* but I can't. I can't get over you." I shouted, my voice cracking somewhere in the middle.
I lifted my head. Carter was gone. It was just me and the wrinkled man at the end of the pier.

I looked out at the water and stared blankly at it. Its rolling blue and grey peaks and valleys. The deep shimmer that went out far across towards the other side. I stood up and walked towards it, putting my hand in the water and feeling the temperature. It was cold.
I hated being cold. But I always felt it. My hands were long and thin and constantly dipped in ice. I used to tell people I had some disease or something that made me cold all the time. That's another reason Winter is so unbearable. But this one in particular. I could feel it coming before the months even started. The inevitable denial of feeling like myself. Another month of feeling like I wasn't where I was supposed to be.

I stared at my open palm in the water and remembered one of the last times I was here with Carter.

I stood up slowly and backed up from the ocean. I closed my eyes and took a breath, searching for that feeling that makes a smile appear on my face. I ran towards the open air and I jumped. I felt the wind whish past my ears and gravity pull me down towards the water. I had a little moment of regret right before I hit the water but it was too late. The weight of the water surrounded me, pulling my body down deep into its clutches as I plunged deeper and deeper, letting the cold liquid surround me. The water chilled me to my core and shocked me enough to make me snap out of my trance. I swam blindly through it towards the surface. I took a big gulp of air and blew bubbles out of my nose. And I swam. Anywhere away from reality. I swam and forgot my fear of the water for a second. I remembered all those times I spent with Carter looking but never going. I plunged back underwater and felt the pressure from the cold marina waters and my drenched shoes surround me like a bubble. It felt good.

I swam around to the other side of the dock and pulled myself up onto a ladder by the private yacht section.

A man with a white coat eyed me suspiciously as I began to ascend the ladder. "Oh no, did you fall in?"

I froze in my tracks at the sound of his voice and smiled awkwardly, letting a puddle of water collect underneath my boots.

"Nope." I said cheekily.

I pulled myself up onto the boards, felling the water weigh me down as I stood up. Wringing out some of the water from my shirt, I walked down the dock slowly towards the fence.

23.

A few hours later

I walked back towards Oja's and picked up my bike by the side. There was no sign of the lady and I didn't bother looking for her just to tell her I didn't have her purse. I pedaled home soaking wet, my teeth chattering uncontrollably. Walking my bike into the garage, the thought of a hot shower was burned into my mind.

The showerhead sputtered to life as I turned it on. The wonderful feeling of the hot water made me stay in until it turned cold.

As I made my way back down the stairs, I saw Sam lounging on the couch in the living room. I asked to see if he got the mail, he shook his head and kept reading.

I walked outside without shoes and opened it up. There was a stack of letters and things. I grabbed the stack in my hand and flipped through. There was a letter for me from a college. I felt a lump form in my throat and I laid the other envelopes back in the mailbox. It wasn't a packet. I knew what it would say before I even opened it, but I let myself open it anyways and be disappointed.

I sat on the curb and let the afternoon cold pour into me. The fog rolled under the darkest parts of my brain and I began drowning in it. Just the same as usual, but somehow worse. This time I had a reason. The first time I got a rejection letter, I expected it. The second time, I wasn't that surprised. But now, my options are dwindling fast. The more no's I get the more horrible I feel.

I heard the crunching of gravel under someone's shoes. Ida walked slowly towards me with a newspaper in her hand and a look of pity on her face.

She sat down next to me. I looked at my hands and pretended I was alone.

"So you didn't get in, huh?" Ida wondered aloud.

I shrugged and gestured to my current state.

"That obvious."

"Yeah."

We got quiet and I heard nature in my thoughts, saw the world from what felt like another bitter and angry body.

"You know, when I started applying to these colleges, I was getting excited thinking about the possibility of just moving away, starting a new life somewhere with people my age. But ever since everything with Carter, I don't really have that feeling anymore. It's just not as fun when you don't have someone to share things with."

Ida hummed in response and I hugged my knees in closer to my body.

"You feel like you're alone, huh?"

"Yeah, I guess."

"That's ok, me too kid. Everybody gets that way sometimes. We can be alone together."

"Really?" I breathed, staring at the ground, only half caring.

"No, I got a thing at three."

"Oh."

"I'm just messing with you. Now come on, let's drink some coffee," she said rising slightly from her position on the curb.

I stayed sitting down as Ida settled back down next to me.

"Ok. I see that look in your eye."

"What?"

"I know you're feeling a lot of stuff right now but that look I see in your eyes right now tells me that you're about ready to give up. And that just can't happen kid."

Ida was my sanity.

"Ida, I've tried so hard to do my best every day of my life for the past seventeen years. And if that's not enough for these colleges then another year of trying is not gonna mean anything."

"Good enough never cuts it kid; you gotta take that and give it everything you got until the very end."

"I think it's too late for that Ida. I've never been very good with initiative. I'll just go to community college."

"Nah. You deserve a better future than that kid."

"Yeah, well, just because I might deserve it doesn't mean I'm gonna get it."

I watched as the sun shone her rays again across the trees and Ida looked up at them sadly.

"You don't have to sit here with me Ida. I'm fine here alone."

"I'm not gonna let you sit here alone on the curb like roadkill Dylan, especially not in this state. Looks like something just died on your face."

"Thanks for that. Anything else uplifting you wanna say?"

"Sure, lots more. Come inside the house. I just made some coffee."

"Really, I'd rather be alone. Your company is not as nice as you think."

"I know you're mad but that was not very nice. Get your ass inside the house, this neighborhood is already depressing enough and your attitude is not helping. Now either come in my house and talk to me or sit out here and sulk until Martha comes home and rages."

Ida and I talked in her kitchen for three hours. She drank almost four cups of black coffee. That cannot be good for a person. After a while of talking about what black holes are and why everyone is obsessed with the hot guy that works at the Stop and Shop, I decided that Ida's exaggerated yawns were my hint to leave.

I warily approached the door to my house, the feeling of my heart beating quickly in my chest making a lump of guilt form in my throat. I hated this feeling, as if getting another rejection letter was my own fault, despite my protests that the schools were too difficult anyway. When I walked in, nobody even bothered to check who it was. My dad was snoring on the couch with a baseball game on to lull him into sleep. Martha was God knows where and Sam was in his room with the door shut, always up to no good.

Love my family.

I opened the door to my room and grabbed the notebook out of my desk drawer as well as a paperclip and three Hershey's kisses. I laid down on my mattress and gingerly unrolled the twine surrounding the notebook. I had remembered something when I was talking to Ida. Something I'd forgotten about a long time ago. A conversation I had in passing with Carter, a suggestion that I was beginning to like very much.

--

"We should do it." Carter said enthusiastically.

I glanced up from my chemistry textbook. "Do what?"

"Yes, we definitely should."

"What are you going on about freak." Carter and I spent hours in the library after school going on and on about what else we could be doing besides geometry.

"Well, as the genius boy I am, I just came up with a brilliant idea.'

"Oh this should be good, what do ya got?"

"This-fog that you're going through, it's mental. Not the British word but like it's in your head, right?" Carter asked innocently.

I nodded and closed my textbook.

"Are we thinking the same thing?"

"Are you thinking of depressing things? Because no, I'm not the one with a mental health problem."

"I was gonna say electroshock therapy."

"That's our backup. Plan A is a little more fun."

"Electroshock therapy isn't fun?"

"Shut up. Here's what I'm thinking. You gotta get out of that head of yours," he pointed out, thumping me playfully on the head with his knuckles. "You're using your thoughts as some sort of playground because you're bored. The simple solution is to get out of town."

"Get out of town?"

"Yeah."

"That's a little cliché, don't you think?"

"Oh it's super cliché, that's why we're *going.*"

"It's a cute idea but we've got a small problem called Martha." I said, turning my finger in a loop beside my head.

"She'll be ok with it the second you mention my name."

"No, not even you can charm my mother into this one."

"You think I'm charming?"

"No."

"Where would we even go?"

"You know that lighthouse I mentioned a while ago?"

"The one up near Dunston."

"Yeah. Well, I was thinking we could drive up there for a few days. Enjoy a part of North Carolina that doesn't suck."
I sighed and bit my tongue.

"What? You don't like it?"

"No, it sounds great but when you said road trip I pictured some place, like, out of North Carolina."

"Like where?"

"I don't know, New York, Philly. Anywhere."

"And you say I'm cliché? We've barely ever left Alliance. This is our chance to find a good place behind all the dilapidated buildings. Plus, your mom is more likely to say yes."
I looked down at my hands on the table, thinking about us traveling somewhere in North Carolina over some city like New York. The bell rang shrilly in my ears and I looked up at Carter.

"Just think about it, let me know what you want after school."

"Not my choice actually."

The door to the library opened and Brady came in with a small parade of his jock friends. They gestured in our direction and Carter and I ran out of the library.

24.
<u>December 9, 2017</u>

I thumb the pages of the notebook between my hands, walking lazily down the crowded streets of downtown. It's so different from our little suburbia I feel like I'm in a completely different part of the world. The buildings are tall and shoved together, the streets narrow and thin. The people almost undoubtedly glaring at me as I walk slowly in front of them on the sidewalk. I used to really love walking with my head up, capturing everything I could through my eyes like a movie. I don't really want to do that anymore.

I'm baffled by my own stupidity sometimes. Baffled by these meaningless and senseless actions that I commit, day after day, week after week. It's the constant tone of adolescence timing in my brain, a tone I thought was knocked out of me that day he died months ago. But just like the Winter, it came creeping back behind my ears. It's that little know nothing attitude that makes me do what I do. Feel what I feel. That cold bitterness that makes me push others away. I want so desperately to love, but I can hardly love myself. And isn't that where it all begins?

I veer right slowly to make my way down towards the water. A man in a business suit and fur coat yells after me, *watch it.* I ignore him and keep walking, clutching the notebook like it's a part of me.

I walk about 40 yards down the gravel path towards the park and water, away from the dead trees and hulking figures, the professionals always in a sort of dramatic hurry. Wearing their busyness like a badge of honor.

I stop and sit on the edge of a park bench, looking out at the world before me. One-part human and the other part nature. Worlds embedded within worlds. And in the middle of it all, me. Me on a park bench surrounded by hundreds of *watch it* people and chill seekers.

I sit here on this bench and just think until I get tired of the waves and the wind and the honking and the confusion. I look out past the tops of the waves and the shrimp boats. Look out past the small children and fake dreams, even past the evening hues of that last bit of light. Look there. Where the color meets and darkness begins to form into shadows, shadows that lurk beneath your feet and claw their way into your heart. It's never been so close before but something must have set it off. This need to get away from my own life.

I shake my head to escape the never-ending path I'm falling down and open up the journal to a random page.

I know it's been only a week since I've written but it feels a lot longer. TJ got in some sort of trouble in Atlanta and the whole family went down for an intervention, even dad. TJ. My brother. That doesn't feel right. A lot has happened. Some good, but mostly bad. The bad ones stick out like sore thumbs in my mind. What does that metaphor even mean?

It's just words on a page, really. Words that even the most lackluster of humans could have written. But somehow they stick to me and I can't get this idea out of my head. And I know that if I don't do it, I will never reach the end of this fog.

--

I waited on the bench for an hour when she showed up, standing in front of me with a bag full of potato chips.

"Hey kid." she greeted.

"Hi, Ida." She sat down next to me on the bench.

"Thanks for meeting me, I'm sure you've got a lot going on at McDonald's."

"Nah, I'm glad you called. I was looking for an excuse to leave today, we just got a shipment of nuggets in and I hate looking at that stuff frozen."

I laughed softly and ran my thumb over the edge of the notebook, looking out across the water.

"So, why are we here kid?"

I sighed and turned slightly to face her.

"I've got something I want to talk to you about."

Ida nodded.

"What do you got for me kid?"

"It's sort of crazy but just hear me out, ok?"

"Well, ok then. Am I allowed to eat my chips while you're talking?"

I shook my head. "If you share."

She smiled and opened up the ziplock.

"Ok. Well, as you know, a lot has happened these past couple of months for me. My best friend, Carter, died in a car crash. That was a few months ago but I still find myself floundering. It's senior year and things are-bad. I'm trying so hard to move on but it's so difficult. My friends, people my age are applying to colleges and getting accepted but I can hardly get out of bed--let alone think about my future away from all of this."

I bit my lip and snuck a glance at Ida, to make sure she was following. Her eyes were half-closed and she seemed to be really listening.

"I'm really sorry about him Dylan. And I want you to know that it's ok to not be able to move on quite yet. Death, passing on, that's a big and terrible thing. No one expects you to get better so soon."

I nodded and looked down at the notebook.

"I'm gonna tell you something that not a lot of people in Alliance know. I used to be married. 29 years."

"What? Why don't you tell people about that?"

She shrugged. "I don't like to dwell on it. You wanna know why?"

"Why?"

"After all these years I still get sad and angry when I think about him. It's been over ten years since he died, Dylan. And I still haven't moved on. Each day gets a little better. But that feeling of sadness, it's very hard to shake."

"Ida, I'm so sorry."

"It's alright kid. But hey look, misery loves company. And if it weren't for our two lovely boys, you and I wouldn't be on this bench together today."

"Wouldn't that be a good thing?"

"Well, I don't think so. I like having you as a friend."

"Me too."

Ida looked out again at the water and I looked at her. Wrinkled and beautiful, strong and supportive. Like a mother should be.

"Well, I didn't bring you out here to make you depressed. I brought you out here to ask you a question. Last Saturday you told me you hadn't left North Carolina in years. Well I haven't either. I figured maybe if I left for a little while, I can clear my head for a minute. Take my mind off of things. I just want to get away. To see what it feels like."

"Well, to be honest with you kid, I don't think you need to leave a place to figure things out. It's not your surroundings, it's you who needs the fixing."

"What do you mean by that."

"You don't need to leave North Carolina to take your mind off things. You need to understand North Carolina, understand yourself."

"But how do I do that?"

"Find what makes you happy and chase after it. You can't be sitting around focusing on how to fight your demons when your demons are all inside of your head, that'll never work. You've gotta get on that bike of yours and escape them."

"Well that's exactly what I would be doing with this trip."

"I love you Dylan, but you shouldn't leave North Carolina. Not yet."

"Well why not?"

"I just told you why not. You can't go be happy somewhere else if you're still unhappy down here."

"I thought you were here to support me."

Ida frowned, the lines in her cheeks creasing sharply against the thin bones in her face. "Don't be that way with me Dylan."

I lowered my head to my hands and set my elbow on my knee, looking out at the water. Ida sighed and laid her hand on my back.

"Listen kid. I'm about to give you some advice. And I don't want you to think I'm trying to harass you or that I'm pushing you. I just want to tell you what I did and see if it works for you."

I sat up and turned my body to face hers.

Ida smiled sadly at me. "If you keep living your life the way you are right now, you will never be able to move on from that boy's death. That I know for sure. The only way you will ever be able to heal is if you try and enjoy life again. You can't expect the pain you feel to go away on its own by sitting around. It'll slowly go away if you restart your life again."

"How?"

Ida shrugged. "Get back in school, for one. Try to get along with everybody. Make compromises, make decisions. Don't let anyone else stand in your way. Fight to get your life back."

I looked Ida in the eye and pursed my lips. "I don't think I can do that right now."

"I didn't think I could either kid. When Bill died, I sat around the house for months. One day I got so sad and weak, I passed out in my front yard on the way to publicly burn my foreclosure notice in the middle of the street. I almost died right there by my witch hazel bush, but someone was there to save me. That's when I realized that I had to get going again. And I'm not gonna lie to you, jumping back in was hard. But it was worth it. Because the more stuff I did, the more people I saw, the less pain I felt."

"You passed out in your front yard?"

She nodded. "Yup. Look kid, I know I give her a bad rap, but North Carolina is not all that bad, it just so happens that you and I chose to live in the worst place here."

"I mean even if that's true, wouldn't it be so much better to leave and go to other places?"

"You really think your mom's gonna let you go?"

I looked down at my lap. "I guess you're right."

We sat down again and watched the boats pass.

"What's that in your hand anyways. You been planning a trip already?"

"No. It's Carter's."

"Oh."

Ida got quiet and we watched as the sun fell lower and lower until there was only the sky in all of its darkness. The streetlamps attracted the bugs but we stayed for a while, enjoying the quiet and the cold and each other's company.

"I'll make you a deal kid. If you go back to school for a few months and you still really hate it. Then I'll take you on that road trip. We can go wherever you want. But for now, I want you to try and go back to school and finish your senior year. It's what Carter would have wanted for you."

We talked and decided on some things, then we left at around two. Ida drove me home. The car was quiet but something felt good in the air, like the wheels were finally turning or something.

It felt as though my whole life leading up to that point wasn't real. Like I had never really been alive until that moment. I was free of the redundancy, free of the pain of being weighed down by my own cowardice to speak up.

Ida pulled up in front of my house and I got out.

"Well, um, I'll see you tomorrow then."

"Tomorrow it is."

"And Ida?"

"Yeah Dylan?"

"Thanks. Really."

"No problem kid."

25.

2 am

I got home and saw that all the lights were on in the house and my family was in the living room.

"Oh my god, she's here." I closed the front door gently and pulled my shoes off, rubbing the sleep out of my eyes to face my family.

"We can see that Martha," my dad snapped. I felt my eyes widen but tried to keep calm. "Dylan, where the hell were you? It's almost two in the morning."

"Where were you?" my mom insisted.

I swallowed the lump in my throat.

"I was at the park."

"What, why?" my dad asked harshly.

"Ida and I were talking."

"Ida? As in our old neighbor Ida?" Martha asked.

"Yes, I asked her to meet me there."

"So you two were at the park for nearly nine hours just talking?" My mom was unconvinced, wrapping her thin robe tighter across her body and getting up to look out the window. Ida was still outside getting out of her car.

"I *was* there for nine hours. Ida met me there after work."

"Is that who you've been spending all your time with? What were you two talking about for so long?"

"Well, I was just about to tell you." I gestured for them to sit down as I settled on the armchair of the couch. My dad opened up his mouth to protest but stopped as I began. "These last few weeks have been very hard. I thought the longer time went on the easier it would be but I was wrong. It's the opposite. The longer I sit and wait for this all to pass the more difficult and depressing my life becomes." I wrung my hands together as I talked, intertwining my pale and thin fingers together in a knot of discomfort and humiliation.

"Sweetie I-" Martha interrupted.

"Please, let me talk. I went to the park to just be alone but the longer I was there, the more I realized how much I hate myself right now. I called Ida because I didn't want to be alone and I realized that I am the weakest when I am by myself. Carter was my only real friend, that was my age anyway, and Ida is the closest person I have to him. We talked and she gave me some much-needed advice about moving on. All this being said, I think it's time I go back to school, stop with all the online school stuff."

I stopped talking and looked at my family from under my eyelashes. They each looked distinctly confused, sad, and agitated. Sam just looked tired.

"I mean, this is a lot to take in," my mom started. "I'm glad you feel ready to tell us those things but are you sure you're ready honey?"

"Yes, this time I'm sure."

Martha and dad exchanged perplexed and angry glances.

"I don't- it's just last week you said you never wanted to go back again and now you're sure you do. I don't want to push you back in there and have another incident on our hands."

"There won't be. I feel ready. I feel like I need to go back now."

"What happened? What changed? Why is talking with Ida any different than talking with Dr. Lupa? What did she say?"

"Dr. Lupa's a counselor. Ida's a friend. There's only so much I can tell Dr. Lupa before it starts to feel weird telling her. Ida knows how I feel and she knows how I can move on."

"If I'd realized Ida would do for free what Dr. Lupa is charging me hundreds for I would have hired her a long time ago."
My mom laughed and my dad stared blankly at her, shaking his head.

"Nice one mom," Sam tried. "Can I go to sleep now?" My dad shook his head at him with a glare and my mom sighed awkwardly.

"You sure that that would help- heal you?" Paul asked.

"Heal? It's not like I'm taking pills here, it's school. It's life, it's-feeling normal again."

"How do you *know* though?" Martha questioned.

"Look, I don't know for sure if going back to school is gonna help. But I know that staying here in this house day after day definitely isn't. I'm gonna be going to college soon and if I don't go back to school now, it's gonna make that transition even harder."

"I'm sorry I just don't understand, why Ida?' My mom tried again.

"She's just always been there."

"Ok."

"What?'

"I said ok."

"Just ok?"

"Well, hold on here Martha." My dad began. "Don't you think we should discuss this in a little more detail first."

"I mean of course you are going to need to give us some specifics and your dad and I will need to lay a few ground rules but I say yes." She replied with a small smile.

"Ok well, we're all tired, so let's get some sleep and we can talk about this more tomorrow." Sam said, already walking slowly for the stairs. I nodded.

"Thanks for caring Sam."

26.
<u>December 16, 2017</u>

There were a lot of discussions after that night. A lot. My parents weren't completely convinced that I was well enough to attend school and neither was the administration of Alliance High. I wasn't really convinced either, but it was something I felt I had to do.

I went over to Ida's a lot for advice and she's probably the only reason all of this is actually happening. My parents and the school board established certain provisions to ensure I wouldn't have any breakdowns. Mandatory meetings with all my teachers, a two-strike limit, a condensed schedule, and an all-access pass to the guidance counselor twice a week. Nevertheless, it worked. Things would soon be back to almost normal.

Through all of this, Ida has been the reason I haven't cracked. Despite how badly I need to be back at school, this constant scrutiny feels almost demeaning and I hate it. Ida has been there.

It's 3 o'clock and I'm shopping for school supplies at Office Depot with Martha. I wanted to go alone with her credit card but she insisted that she had to go too. I'm staring at a pack of 12 number 2 pencils and I can't help but feel strange.

"What about this one?' Martha says holding up a brightly colored spiral 3-ring binder with a pink and blue pattern on the front.

"Really?" I asked with a raised eyebrow.

"Ok, I'm only half kidding."

I browsed the aisle full of fresh paper and ran my hand along the metal structures holding them.

"I didn't think I'd be doing this again," Martha said, eyeing a pack of highlighters and tossing them in the basket she had tucked on her elbow.

"No?"

"Yeah. With Sam being in college and you a senior. You guys have both grown up right under my nose."

I eyed her strangely. She never was one for nostalgia but she was smiling right now. Thinking.

"People grow up. It happens. Doesn't mean we still can't go shopping together."

"Yeah, I know."

We turned a corner into the pen and marker isle and I tried to keep the conversation going, just to see where it would take us. "I'm surprised Sam even let you go shopping with him. He's so entitled I figured he'd insist on paying for things himself."

My mom laughed softly. "Sam loves you, you know. I know it may not seem like he cares sometimes, but he does. Teenage boys are just bad at showing it." she said as she picked up a pack of erasers and threw them in the cart. I felt reassured by her comment about Sam.

"Is that why you wanted to come today?"

"Huh?"

"Is that why you're shopping for school stuff with me? Cause you feel like Sam and I won't want to do stuff with you soon?"

"Yes and no. You're my kid. It's what moms should do."

I opened my mouth to make a snide remark but decided to just keep my mouth shut. I didn't want to be the one that started the fights.

"Yeah."

We spent a hundred dollars on school supplies and got Burger King value menu for lunch on the way home.

When we got back to the house I went to my room and listened to the Shins for a while. After about an hour I grabbed my bag with Carter's journal in it and ran down the stairs again heading towards the front door.

"Where you going sweetie?" my mom asked. I turned around and saw my mom and my dad sitting at the table, both drinking sprites out of cans. That's new.

"Ida's."

"Why don't you stay here tonight. Hang out with us," my dad suggested between awkward sips of his Sprite. I looked at them with my mouth slightly opened, confused about whether or not this was a serious offer.

"Uh, really?" I asked, walking towards the kitchen table.

"Yeah. We can play a card game or watch a movie if you want. Your pick." he said. I looked over at my mom and she shot me an encouraging smile.

"Oh, sure. That sounds nice." I stammered with a smile. And I really mean it too. I hung my bag and my hat on the railing of the stairway and walked over to my parents, taking a seat between them at the table. I could hear the voice of Daniel Pitts on the tv in a commercial for an action movie. My mom didn't even seem to notice.

27.
January 8, 2018

Christmas was the best holiday we'd had together in years. Martha wasn't drunk, my dad actually made a joke, and Sam actually talked to us. It all came and went so fast, like time was trying to get me back to my life as quickly as possible.

"I hate that hat," Martha said with a smile. "You never let me wash it."

"I know, that's why I'm wearing it away from you." I said laughing. My dad and brother came out of the house together. I saw Ida leaning over the railing of her porch with some slippers on and a cup of steam making her glasses fog up.

"Here let me help you with that," Sam offered as I tried to grab my bike off the rack in the garage.

"Thank God I was about to break every bone in my body lifting that thing." I said jokingly. I rubbed my hands together in the cold January air.

My mom and dad stood in front of me. Paul had his hands shoved awkwardly in his pockets, Martha with a guilty half-smile on her face. After a minute of us huddled together with our teeth chattering, Martha spoke.

"So, are you excited?"

"Um, yeah. I mean it's school but I'm ready."

"I hope so sweetie."

"Remember to be smart," my dad added. "Always be alert, looking out for creeps in the halls. If anyone gives you trouble call us immediately."

"Dad, I'll be fine. I'm actually very capable. And it's high school by the way, not prison."

"Are you sure you want to take your bike sweetie? I can drop you off." my mom asked as Sam came up behind me with my bike.

"I'll be fine. I wanna do this on my own."

"Worst comes to worst Paul," Ida started yelling from her porch. "I got us each some pepper spray from the drug store. She'll be ready if any kid tries to jump her."

I laughed and Ida cackled, the rest of my family managing a few fake giggles. I picked my book bag up off the ground.

"Alright, well, give me a hug!" Sam said to me. I squeezed him tightly and wondered why this was happening.

"Don't accept any drugs!" he encouraged as he patted me on the back.

I hugged Paul next. "Don't take *any* drugs!" he said.

"I'll use my best judgment on that one dad, don't worry."

I hugged Martha as Sam and my dad started back for the house, each of them jogging in to keep warm. She looked at me with a small smile and her arms wrapped tightly around herself. I hopped on my bike and slung my book bag over my shoulders. As I pulled away, she grabbed onto my arm.

"Hey, wait."

I stopped.

"What?"

She gently tucked a stray piece of hair behind my ear and smiled, rubbing my left shoulder comfortingly.

"I just wanted to say, I hope that going back to school helps. I hope you find yourself again, I know you will. And when you come home, we're here to support you. And we're gonna be better for you. We're gonna be a better family."

I held her gaze and squeezed her hand.

"Thanks Mom. For everything."

"Proud of you."

I pedaled out of the driveway and waved to my parents. I felt like a kindergartener on their first day of school. I hiked my book bag up higher and saw Ida sitting on her porch with her wine. She waved and blew a kiss.

--

I smiled as a breeze made the branches of the trees wave at me as I passed by. It was reassuring to my nervous bones. I pulled around the corner and saw the school, already the outlines of cars taking up most of the view of the parking lot. I pulled into the lot and walked my bike towards a bike rack, locking my blue ride onto the middle rack. I watched as a few kids made their way into the building. It was a big school so I didn't know most of the faces. I had been put into classes at the beginning of the second semester so at least I wasn't walking in completely blind somewhere in the middle. I glanced at the folded paper in my hand and ran over my small schedule again in my head. I had done a lot of online classes and the principal is only letting me take what I need to graduate.

First class: Probability and Statistics. Second: Chemistry. Third: English 4. Then lunch, meet with a counselor, home. I leave school every day by 1:30. Not much different than my skip days.

A guy in a green beanie held open the door for me and I managed to mumble a small thanks. I looked cautiously across the long and ill-lit hallway that seemed to go for miles in one endless direction. A mass of students ran in every direction towards class. It felt weird being back. It had only been four months since I had left but it felt like an eternity. I walked close to the lockers and turned left into the main office. The receptionist looked up at me with a faint smile. I assumed she didn't recognize me.

"Hi. Can I help you with something?"

"Uh, yes. I was told to meet Principal Newport here in the morning."

"Of course." She typed some things into her computer and looked back up at me. "Dylan?"

"Yes."

"Alright, Dylan. You can head on back to his office. Third door on the left."

I knocked softly as I approached Principal Newport's door and he waved me in from behind the glass window. I stepped through and nodded at a man who was just leaving.

"I'll call you when I get the final draft. Thanks, Mark."

The man nodded as he brushed past me and I closed the door behind him.

"Good morning Dylan, have a seat." he said, gesturing to the small wooden chair that sat in front of his desk.

I sat down and eyed Principal Newport as he made his way around his desk. I never really liked the guy. He was tall and pudgy with a mean looking face. His dark hair was thinning at the top and his frown lines were deeply rooted into his pale cheeks. He reminded me of some sort of retired politician with an eating habit.

"Morning Mr. Newport."

"Thanks for taking the time to meet with me before class. I just wanted to reiterate a few things before you head out."

I nodded with tight lips and laid my bag down on the floor. I decided to keep my mouth shut so I wouldn't give him a reason to kick me out.

"Of course."

Newport rolled his chair up to his computer, his big belly preventing him from rolling up to a certain point. He typed quickly on the keyboard and snuck glances at me from behind the screen.

I looked around with slight disgust at his office. He was a disorganized man with piles of folders and papers surrounding him. He had pictures of him hunting covering the wall as well as a degree from some college that I'd never heard of. He cleared his throat and wheeled back.

"Well, everything looks good here, your profile is all up to date. I have a new schedule for you, however, to fit your class requirements. Some of the classes you took online didn't come through until a week after we gave you the old schedule." I looked down at the folded sheet of paper in my hand and put it in the pocket of my book bag. Principal Newport rolled over to the printer and handed me a new slip of paper. I scanned the list and nodded. Chemistry, Batts. Probs and Stats, LeClair. Literature, Fitz. No.

"Oh, um, I think this is a mistake. I had Mr. Fitz for English last year."

"Oh, yes. He teaches senior English as well this year."

"Uh, is there any other teacher I could have?"

"No, I'm afraid this is the only English class left for you to take. All the others are full."

I bit my lip and felt my leg start to bounce.

"Would there be a problem between you and Mr. Fitz?"

"No, no problem. Just wondering."

"Ok, great. Now that you have your new schedule I'd just like to remind you…" I listened with my eyes as Newport kept babbling on about behavior and the opportunities I had here to receive help. All I could think about was kicking my foot in Mr. Fitz's stomach. Finally, after what felt like hours of Newport talking at me, I opened the door to the main hallway and headed down towards the stairwell.

--

I had almost finished my first day and it wasn't completely terrible. The worst class was yet to come. Mr. Fitz's. I walked down the hall and up the stairs to his hallway. As I approached I was happy to not be seeing him leaning against his doorway like he usually does. It was like some sort of weird intimidation technique. I breathed a little better as I approached his door.

"Dylan."

I lifted my head at the sound of my name and felt my eyes widen slightly. It was Mr. Fitz. He was just leaving the open door of his classroom.

"Oh. Mr. Fitz." I eyed him cautiously and took slow steps backward. "I was just leaving." Crap, why did I say that?

"Oh. I didn't realize you were back."

"Yeah. Today's my first day."

He nodded. "Oh. How are you?"

"Good. I don't know why I said I was leaving I'm actually in your class." Nice.

"Oh, great. Well, come on in."

I eyed him cautiously as I made my way in through his door, taking my usual seat to the left near the back. I plopped down in my desk and tried to contain my annoyance at everything.

"Dylan?"

God not again. I turned my head and was met with a half-familiar face. It was this guy who was in my class last year. A tall guy with thick black hair and pale skin. He had a wonky smile on his face that reminded me of Ida.

"Oh hey, Peter right?"

"Yeah. Looks like we both got Fitz again."

"Yeah."

He leaned in and gestured towards the door. "I hate this guy. He's a terrible grader."

I breathed out slowly and leaned in too. "Right? God, I'm so glad you said that. I thought I was the only one."

"Nah, he's the worst."

I nodded and put my bag on the back of my chair. I looked over at Peter's desk again and saw his notebook had a sticker on it.

"You like them?" I asked.

Peter looked down at his notebook with a picture of The Shins on it and smiled at me. "Yeah. I like them a lot. I saw them in a concert over break."

"Me too. Well, it was a while ago though."

"Really? You got a favorite song?"

"Simple Song probably. What about you?"

"Me too." I smiled and he smiled back and I suddenly felt myself breathe a little easier. It felt nice to have someone my age to relate to again, and not to mention find refuge during Mr. Fitz's class. I found it difficult to pay attention during class but I took all the notes I could. His voice alone made me want to spit at him. I looked over at Peter and he rolled his eyes. I wondered why I had never talked to him before.

I grabbed my bag as the bell rang and started to leave class.

"See you tomorrow Dylan," Peter crooned as he grabbed his notebook off his desk. "You'll be here tomorrow, right?"

"Yeah. You can't get rid of me that easy Peter."

"Good," he said as he turned with a smile. I smiled back and tried to walk past Fitz, stopping in my tracks at the door.

"Hey, Mr. Fitz." I said. He turned towards me with a grimace. "I'm sorry about what I said last year. I hope that we can have a fresh start this semester."

He stood up a little straighter and eyed me cautiously. "Sounds good Miss. Anderson."

I wasn't convinced and neither was he.

28.
February 7, 2018

The next few weeks were fairly uneventful. I went to Dr. Lupa's only once a week now. I went through each class with the same enthusiasm every other person did, paying half attention and doing classwork. I never raised my hand and no one ever called on me which was nice. I hadn't seen Brady yet and Kaylee and Maya left me alone, choosing to keep their distance and merely sneer at me in the hallway.

I spend most of the day waiting for it to be over. I don't really skip anymore which is new. Maybe it's because my favorite class is at the end of the day. With Peter. It doesn't hurt that I get B's in Fitz's class now, even though some of my papers are carbon copies of the ones I did last year.

Today was my fifth Wednesday at school and my fourth Wednesday eating lunch with Peter.

"So who do you usually sit with?"

Peter looked up from his tray. "Hmm? Oh, well last semester I sat with Kyle, Luke and Brady. That whole bunch."

I swallowed at the mention of Brady's name. "Oh. I didn't know you guys were friends."

"Uh, yeah. Our relationship has always been a bit strained."

"What do you mean?" I hope he meant to say nonexistent.

"Well, Brady and I were best friends in middle school. He was a great kid back then. But when high school started, he became someone completely different, at least around other people. And it sucks because here at school he's an asshole, to be blunt, but when it's just him and I he's a good guy. The guy I remember being friends with. And because he still has that side of him, I've been reluctant to break it off."

"Wow. Brady Dean, a good guy. I never would have guessed. How come I never see the two of you hanging out?"

"I've never been a great hang out guy. I don't mind being by myself sometimes. I think that's why Brady and I's friendship works, because he only has to be a good guy 10% of the time."
I laughed and nodded, taking a small bite of my turkey sandwich.

"I'm glad you saved me from that."
I looked up at him slowly and smiled with my teeth. "Me too. You deserve better." Peter nodded slowly and looked out across the cafeteria.
He turned his head slowly back at me, his brown eyes shining under the glare of the cafeteria lights. "What are you doing Friday?"

"Friday? I'll be at school."

"No, I mean after."
I felt color rise slowly into my cheeks. "Oh, nothing right now."

"Well good. We're going to a movie."
My eyes widened slightly. "We are? Aren't you going to actually ask me first?"

"No, because then there's a chance of you saying no." He said with a sort of shy confidence about him.
I laughed. The bell rang.

"I'll check what's playing tonight and text you."

"Ok."
He hopped off the tall stool at the table and we walked together to throw away our trash.

"See you tomorrow?"

"See you tomorrow." I said, watching him walk away to class. I have a date.

29.

Later that day

Friday was in two days. I had two days of thinking about going on a date with a boy named Peter who is in my English class and likes the Shins. This was going to be rough. After school I decided to head to O'Malley's, I needed some serious help. And this time, I didn't mean psychological.

I walked in and set my bag behind the podium by the entrance. I don't ever have to check if Sawyer is working because she always is, I'd be shocked if one day her name wasn't on the schedule at least seven times in one week.

Sure enough, she was smoking a cigarette with Carlos in the back. They hastily put out their cigarettes and fanned the room when they saw me.

"Oh my gosh, baby, give us some warning."

"You guys know I'm seventeen, right?"

Carlos shrugged and threw his cigarette out the back door, wiping his hands off on his apron.

"Why do you guys smoke back here? The door is literally five feet away, everyone can smell it."

Carlos shrugged. "Always smells smoky anyways. We burn everything."

I rolled my eyes and sat down on the stool by the sink, Sawyer smiled at me and reached her arms out for a hug, the smell of nicotine hung on her like a coat of perfume on a rich woman.

"What can we do for you today sugar bug?"

"Yeah sugar bug," Carlos teased, imitating Sawyer's thick southern accent. She swatted at him playfully with a dish rag.

"It's kind of embarrassing. But I need some motherly advice." I murmured, looking back and forth between the two. Carlos looked confusedly at Sawyer and she looked back at him with an expression that read leave us alone now idiot. He did not understand.

"Ok sugar. Follow me to my office. Carlos, call me if any tables come in."

"Wait-what? Oh, I get it. Don't worry Sawyer, there won't be." Sawyer pulled me gently by my hand into Pete's office. The room was covered with cutouts of Lauren Bacall and ladies from department store magazines. Boxes from pizza places and sandwich shops covered the desk and the computer screen was hardly readable with all the smudges covering the screen.

"Oh God, how does he live like this?" My eyes caught the sight of a paper bag from Taco Bell and I felt myself linger on it. It's funny how nostalgic a little bag of fast food can make me feel.

"He doesn't live here. I wish he did though. Without Pete it's just four people to run the place. And we can't do much."

"Wait, where'd he go?"

"Bypass surgery. Said he'd be back in a couple of days."

"Oh."

"Anyways, what advice do you need? I'm dying for some girl talk."

"Oh, yeah. Well, what I'm about to tell you is very middle school but I just needed to ask somebody."

"That's what I'm here for sugar."

"This guy in my English class, Peter. We've been talking and-"

"Wait, English class? When did you start school again?"

"Oh, I don't know, two weeks ago. Anyways, Peter and I were in the same class last year but I didn't start talking to him until now. I got to know him-"

"You didn't even notice him last year? That sounds a little fishy to me baby."

"No, it's fine. My attention was on--other people at the time. So, we've been talking and I found out he's a lot like me. He likes the Shins, he hates Mr. Fitz."

"Who's Mr. Fitz?"

I stared at Sawyer and sighed. "Can you let me talk? Or should I leave?"

"Don't get all sassy girl. I'll stay quiet."

"Ok, thank you. We're a lot alike and we've been talking and he wants to take me to a movie on Friday."

Silence.

"Ok now you have nothing to say?"

"Well, I'm waiting. Is that it?"

"Yes! I've never been on a date before!"

"You're kidding me, right?"

"No, I'm not."

"Honey, you've been on plenty of dates. You went on some right here in this restaurant."

"What are you talking about?"

"I'm talking about you and that Carter boy." I felt my body go rigid at the mention of his name.

"What? No. Those weren't dates, Sawyer. We were best friends."

"Hmm." Sawyer leaned back in Pete's chair and pursed her lips, staring at me like she was thinking hard about something.

"What's that look for?"

"Honey, I've been on plenty of dates in my day. And if that boy wasn't in love with you, then I don't know what love is anymore."

I stared at her in the dim lighting of Pete's office. I let the smell of burnt food and nicotine fill into every pore of my body and I sat there thinking. I didn't really feel any emotion right then, I was only conscious of the fact that that was the first time someone mentioned Carter in a casual conversation. And the first time anyone's ever told me anything about love in a long time.

"Baby? You alright?"

I blinked a few times and sniffed. "Yeah, I'm fine. Thanks for the advice Sawyer. I'll see you soon."

She voiced some sort of goodbye as I walked out the door, waving bye to Carlos as I picked up my bag in the front.

30.
<u>Feb. 8, 2018</u>

I rode my bike to Ida's house with Carter's notebook. I'd been slowly trying to read some chapters with her, hoping that ultimately finishing the book would bring me peace rather than pain. And sharing either of those emotions with another person is better than doing it all by yourself.

I put my bike by the garage and went into her house. She greeted me with her sweatpants on and a stick of incense burning in her hand. She set it down in a bowl as we made our way to her kitchen where she had the coffee waiting.

I pulled the notebook out of my bag and put it between the two of us. We were on an entry from April 15th, three days after his 18th birthday. I read his birthday entry by myself last week. I didn't want Ida to see me ugly cry like I did. This was the next entry he had written.

April 15th, 2017

Today was a lot different than the past week, not the good kind. I went to buy a pack of cigarettes at the gas station behind Laurel Hill. I thought I could leave them on TJ's windshield as a joke. He hates smoking. Anyways, it was mid-day when I got there. I could still see the track marks from Dylan's bike from my birthday in the grass.

I bought a pack of Newport's, the cheapest, and went to leave out the back. I heard two guys talking by the dumpsters, where no one could see them. It was Brady. I thought he was picking on some kid so I went to help him. Turns out they were just talking. It seemed serious so I tried to sneak away, but it was too late.

Before I know what's happening, Brady's got me on the ground. He starts kicking me really hard in the stomach, over and over, asking me if I was listening to them. I didn't hear anything really but he kicks me a couple more times for good measure. I looked up just as they were leaving and I see the guy he was talking to, I recognize him, I know him from school. I didn't realize he was one of them. He took my cigarettes. Happy birthday to me.

"That's messed up," Ida said. "Brady's in a lot of these. He sounds like the worst kid ever." I nodded and listened to her as she talked about whether or not it was ethical to hire a hitman to kill an eighteen-year-old. I listened sort of. But I was mostly wondering who the other kid in the journal was.

31.

Feb. 9, 2018

Peter and I talked at school, agreeing that he'd pick me up at my house around six to go to the roller rink. My idea, of course. I went home after Mr. Fitz's and sat in my room waiting for 5:25, a time I felt was acceptable enough to start getting ready so I didn't sit around looking good for no reason.

I decided to wear jeans and a cute purple shirt. At exactly six I heard a knock at my door. I ran down the stairs, yelling at Martha that I was leaving for the night. I grabbed my hat off of its hook by the door out of habit and stared at it for a second in my hand. I'd worn it every day for so long that it felt strange to leave without it. Reluctantly, I put it back on its hook and opened up the door, the memory of the hat on my head making my scalp feel tingly and my head feel dizzy.

"Good evening Dylan," Peter said amusedly, making me forget about that hat as I focused on his face. "Peter," I replied as I followed him down to his car. He left his green minivan in the middle of the road. My other neighbor was having people over and there were no spaces to park. "I hope you're a better skater than parallel parker." I said jokingly.

"Oh, don't worry. I'm not."

--

I watched as Peter skated around the rink, falling constantly but getting back up again. I laughed and clapped each time he did it. It was half me thinking it was funny and half me feeding his ego. I'm just a good person like that. I teased him as he kept falling and he seemed to thrive off of it.

It was a busier night than usual for the rink. People who didn't all look like murderers were skating around us. Peter spun me around as Britney Spears started singing to us through the large speakers. I laughed and laughed for a long time and felt happy for a moment. It was really nice.

I saw Rosie watching me out of the corner of my eye and I glanced in her direction. She smiled at me softly and I smiled back. Maybe she was thinking what I was thinking. That seeing Peter stumble around the rink like that felt oddly familiar. I glanced at the bulletin board by the entrance to the rink. Some of Carter's pictures were still there but most of them were covered with flyers for a new car dealership.

--

As he drove me home, I suddenly felt this guilty feeling rise up within me. An uncomfortable feeling that made me squirm a little in my seat. I realized that I had found somebody like Carter. Almost like a replacement. I was trying to find a carbon copy of my old best friend, not anyone new. I looked over at Peter and all I could think about was how much I wish it were him. That was selfish. I wondered if I would feel like that my whole life anytime I met a guy.

Peter pulled up in front of my house a little past ten. I saw the light on in the living room.

I looked over at him and smiled. He smiled back and held my gaze. I felt him lean in and the sounds on the radio got quiet, my breathing slowed to a stop.

"Stop," I said suddenly. I felt my cheeks get red and I felt even worse. I wanted to kiss him but it all felt wrong.

"What's wrong?" he asked, clearly reading the distress on my face.

"Um, there's something on your face." I said. Really Dylan? Oh man. He went to look in the rearview mirror but I stopped him. "Wait, I'll get it."

I opened up his glove box, rummaging around for some sort of napkin to wipe off the imaginary piece of nothing and then have to figure stuff out from there. I decided I'd probably just run out of the car.

My eyes lingered on something in the glovebox. A pack of Newport cigarettes. I pulled them out and Peter's eyes widened.

"Oh, I don't really smoke," he said. He averted his eyes as he said it.

"You don't, do you?"

"No, I swear. I bought those when I turned eighteen. You know, a novelty gift for myself."

"For you, huh? Are you sure these weren't meant for somebody else?"

"What are you talking about?"

"Did you take these from Carter Higgins?"

Peter looked at me guiltily and hesitated. "Yes. I did."

"You did?" I could feel the anger rise up in me. I threw the pack of cigarettes at Peter's chest and got out of the car, slamming the door behind me.

"Dylan wait," Peter yelled, coming around his car and grabbing me by the arm.

"Don't touch me," I yelled. "Asshole. Did you invite me to hang out just so you could make fun of me with Brady? Is that it?" I could feel the hot tears running down my face. It made me realize how cold it was outside. I put my arms around myself.

"What? No, no, Dylan. It's not like that. I would never do that to you. I wanted to hang out with you because I like you."

"Really? You like me? I don't believe you. Why else would you keep the fact that you and Brady beat people up for fun a secret." I turned to go into my house but Peter stood in front of me.

"Please Dylan, just listen. I don't do that. That's just Brady. When people first told me about him doing that, I didn't believe them. Or at least, I didn't want to. That day with Carter was the first time he had done that in front of me. When I saw what he did, I felt so guilty and angry. I broke it off with him right then."

"When you *saw* what he did to Carter? You were right *there* Peter. You could have stopped him. Instead, you stood by and watched like a coward, then you stole his dumb cigarettes before you left. That's pathetic. You're no better than Brady."

"I'm sorry Dylan. I was surprised, I was frozen. He started punching him out of nowhere. I learned so much shit about what Brady had done that day, I realized I'd been trying to hold onto someone that Brady wasn't anymore. And I only took the cigarettes because I thought he was gonna start smoking and shit. My dad's a smoker and it sucks. I didn't think about it being his birthday and all." I shook my head.

"Wait, before you go back in your house and never speak to me again, you gotta know something."

"What."

"Before we knew Carter was in the gas station, Brady told me something. About TJ. You know how he got arrested in Atlanta?" I nodded slowly. "What's that gotta do with this?"

"It wasn't TJ's weed. It was Brady's."

"What? Brady and TJ barely know each other."

"Yes, they do. Brady and TJ went to Atlanta together for the weekend. TJ thought it was just to have fun but it wasn't just that. Brady was trying to sell to some guy down there. When they were caught, it was TJ's car it was found in. He automatically got in trouble and Brady walked."

"Why would TJ take the fall for that?"
He shrugged. "Maybe he felt ashamed for having trusted Brady in the first place. I know I do."

"Why would he tell you all this?"

"I told you, Brady and I were friends. And he likes to brag."

"Why didn't you tell anybody?"

"I wanted to. But I didn't think it was my place. I figured, if TJ wants people to know the truth, he'll tell the truth."

"You should tell TJ that you know. Let him know he's got someone on his side."

"That was almost a year ago. Wouldn't it be too late?"

"It's never too late." I said.

"Is it too late for me and you?"

I looked at him seriously with the pack of Newport's in his hand and his apologetic green eyes.

"I don't know yet." And I went inside. My mom glanced at me as I walked in and started to ask how it went, but I'm sure the answer was all over my face.

32.

<u>That night</u>

It was a nightmare, I'm sure of it now. The colors too vibrant, the feelings too strong. Over Exaggerated and taunting. It couldn't have been real; the smell was putrid and intoxicating and vile. Citrus and pure hatred. From my imagination somewhere behind all that moss and blank thoughts. I thought I'd hidden down below in my mind, somewhere my subconscious could never find it.

All that red.

That color red hadn't existed until that moment. It was thick and glossy and everywhere. A delicate shower of cherry red petals covered every inch of the forest floor. I laid a shaky hand on a vine, pale and purple with the cold. I half expected it to turn to a pale dust on my fingers.

The color felt like what you'd expect. Rough and scaly like the bark on that big tree in my backyard from years ago. A simple branch on a nothing tree. Thousands of red, citrus giants forming a thick ravine. A bloody ravine that could swallow me. "Wow," I remarked under my breath. I felt like the way a twelve-year-old boy does watching his sister's friend get off her motorcycle in skinny jeans. Despite all of those feelings it evoked, something about it made it seem, I don't know. Happy? Comforting?

Strange.

It was in the way the sun bounced off the trees and made the forest floor bathe in a faint yellow light. It was in the way the breeze made the leaves sway in a lazy rhythm that made it hard to keep my eyes open. It was in the way I was with you here on a Tuesday afternoon on an unlikely kind of day that I thought was going to be one of those days that you hate for no reason other than it's a Tuesday and every Tuesday has been the same for the last two years. I don't know exactly what it was, but I liked it. I wanted all of it.

I snuck a glance in your direction and you smiled your smile back. "Let's get closer."

We walked deeper into the red collection, taking in that familiar foreign smell and red mist. We let the trees swallow us and the ever-shrinking path squeeze us together until your hand started brushing against mine. That's so stupid. That was the most unreal part of all of it. I hate dreams. I hate seeing and being with what I can't have. I hate waking up just when it starts to get really good.

I let the red pull us in, closer. The vines tangling around us to form some sort of canopy protecting my white skin. The ground cool and damp around my sneakers.

"Are you angry with Peter?" I asked, smoothing a small petal between my thumb and middle finger.

You laughed gently, focusing his gaze on the tall red vines. "Of course not."

You laughed your laugh and your hand brushed against mine again, lingering. "Are you mad at me?"

I looked at you shyly from under a dark haze of my purple hat. I stopped to stare at your face beneath a patch of sun. "No. Why would I be?"

He frowned. "Because I left you all alone in the world."

I shook my head and smiled sadly. "I'm not alone."

"Yes, you are. I'm the only one who ever really loved you."

I stepped away from Carter and pursed my lips. "That's not true."

He looked back at me with a blank expression. "Yes it is."

I grimaced and folded my arms, no longer liking the dream I was in. "You don't mean that. This isn't even real. Look around you! Look *at* you!" I urged, gesturing to the red forest and poking you sharply in the ribs.

You jumped and laughed your laugh. I gasped at that sound. That was the only real thing about all of this. Your laugh was your laugh. I scoffed and giggled slightly in spite of it all. Taking one of my hands, you stepped close and held a red petal on my nose, tickling me slightly.

I frowned and closed my eyes, wishing I could be content for a moment. "I wish this was real," I hummed quietly.

I opened my eyes slowly, expecting to see my yellow wallpaper and old stuffed friends. I struggled to open my eyes, my body stuck halfway between my dream and my reality. My little green discs were met with an unimaginable amount of red. The walls red. The vines red. The sounds red. The sky red. Your lips red. The world red.

33.
<u>February 12, 2018</u>

There are times in life when things pile up. You can only drag your problems behind you in a little black bag for so long before they get ahead of you. Start taking over you a little, make you crazy. It's hard. But you don't have to care

The dream stayed with me throughout the weekend, wondering what it all meant and who Peter really was. I locked myself in my room for the last two days to just think. But today was school.

The hall was thick with grumbling students, like a never-ending fog across a graveyard. Somber and loud with dirty jokes and frequent stares into the void of the general population.

The lights are blinding, the glare embedding itself under my right eye. I push ahead past the open lockers and loud talkers, the sound of over-chewed and flavorless gum being popped over and over again. People gathered in clusters across the hall. I pushed past, pretending they were nothing but imaginary. *Don't get in your head. Don't get in your head. Feel that anger? That's real, that's what you feel. You feel real. You are real. He is not real. Not anymore.*

My eye twitched at the sight of every perfect and expensive looking person. I wanted to rip everyone to shreds. If it weren't for the fact that I felt obligated to come here, I would have skipped. But something told me I had to come to school today.

Another day of sluggishly moving down the long hallways full of meaningless people and meaningless conversations, what was the point anymore? Tomorrow I would wake up and I would be the same, do the same, feel the same. Dead and tired, not seeing the point, not knowing the answer. A wise woman once told me that if I didn't like something, I could either start to like it or stop doing it. So, I had a choice to make.

I made it almost all the way through the day. I wasted every class impatiently tapping my foot and staring at a spot on the wall. And now I was in Mr. Fitz's. I was reluctant to face Peter. I prepared to ignore him all class, but he didn't show up. I looked longingly at his empty seat.

I hadn't showered all weekend, I'd worn the same outfit since last Friday. Black rings of sleeplessness hung like dead men around my eye sockets. It felt strange being surrounded by the unaffected people around me. Had they ever felt this way? What are they thinking? Do they care? Did they remember him?

My eyes were glued on the clock every second of that class. That's all I'd ever paid attention to anymore, time. How slow it is, how made up it seems to be.

"Dylan."

My eyes shifted slowly and bored towards the front of the room. Mr. Fitz. The kind of teacher that's balding and bitter about it, taking it out on the clueless kids. Never really teaching, just lecturing and cramming information into our brains like robots.

"Ah good, now that you're done nodding off, do you mind answering the question?"

I didn't blink and sunk lower in my chair, feeling my stomach twist into knots in my fury and embarrassment. I shook my head and tried to stare back at the window by the clock.

"What did I say?" he asked. I jiggled my leg impatiently and gritted my teeth. Decisions, decisions.

"I don't know." I half-whispered.

"What?"

A few people giggled and I held back.

"I said I don't know."

"This is an AP class, Dylan. You either need to start paying attention and lose the attitude or switch out of my class."
My mind was made up.

"Fuck you." I snapped blatantly.

"Excuse me?"

"I said fuck it!" I stood up and slung my backpack over my shoulder, standing in front of the class.

"You all are some of the worst people I've ever met in my life. It has been so bad sitting next to you people for the last ten years. Except for you Jason. And you Molly. But to everyone else, *fuck you!*"

"Miss. Anderson, sit back down now. I'm calling an administrator."

"No need Mr. Fitz, I was just on my way out. Before I do go though, let me just say you are still an asshole. I mean, God, I don't think I've met a more insensitive man in my entire life."
Mr. Fitz's cheeks reddened and he made a move towards the phone on his desk. The class squirmed awkwardly in their seats, some of them slyly taking a video from under their desk.

"Now listen-"

"No, you listen. I'm a human being, I have a *life*. Surprise! I know that's a new thing for you. You all wanna know what's been happening in my life recently? My best friend *died* a couple months ago. Yeah. Maybe you would have known if any of you gave a crap about anyone but yourselves. It was a car crash, some idiot hadn't gotten the memo about texting and driving. He died *suffering.*" I felt tears flooding into my eyes but I didn't stop there.

"Losing him is hard, but continuing to live in this place without him is even worse. I can't wake up from this nightmare that I'm stuck in, knowing that someone so smart and so incredible is gone and no one seems to notice. So you'll forgive me if I haven't been doing my homework, Mr. Fitz. Sorry I've been too preoccupied mourning the only person to me that matters."

I stopped yelling and looked around the class. Each row of desks covered with the faces of its stunned and confused students. Mr. Fitz on the phone calling an administrator. Time slowing down. I slowly backed out of the room and ran down the hall.

I ran out of the room as fast as I could I turned down the hallway and saw someone in the distance at the end of the hallway. Brady. Oh God.

I opened up my locker calmly and tried to wait till he left.

I hid my face in my locker for as long as I could but knew eventually I'd have to suck it up and move on before the administrator came looking for me.

Finally, I mustered up the courage and closed it. Brady stared at me from across the hall. I knew it. My luck sucks.

I tried walking away but he ran up to me. He grabbed my arm and I wrestled it away. "Get away from me asshole."

He whistled through his teeth and I grimaced, glancing around us in the hallway looking for a way out. "Where you going in such a hurry Anderson? Trying to run away from yourself?"

"Funny. Actually just getting out of school but thanks." I said as he walked slowly towards me again. I feeling of the cool metal doors of lockers rubbed up against my back giving me déjà vu of the last time we talked.

"Oh, don't do that. Not when I just got you alone."

"Wow you really are a charmer but I'm in a rush and I've got to get going." I fumed, lifting myself off the lockers. Brady pushed me harshly back onto them.

I narrowed my eyes. "Don't push me right now Brady."

I felt his face inch closer to mine as his smirk grew wider and wider. The angry vortex growing in the pit of stomach throbbed with intensity as I felt his face inch closer to me again. I drew back my head further from his and slammed it forward, making Brady stagger backward in shock. He grunted as I stumbled out of his way and into the middle of the hall.

"You know Brady, I feel sorry for you. Which is weird for me by the way." I admitted as Brady sat down on the ground clutching his forehead. "Despite your constant bullying and asshole-ness, I feel sorry for you because I know that you can't help it, it's just who you are. You don't learn your lesson. You'll always and forever be nothing more than a pretentious high school idiot. And with that in mind, I am telling you now that I forgive you. Don't take that for granted because you probably don't deserve it. But I'm forgiving you today with the hope that I too can be undeservedly forgiven for everything I'm about to do." I vented, picking up my bag off the floor, my eyes still blurring slightly from the force of my head-butt.

"Try not to mess with people so much Brady. It'll only get you hurt. Have a nice life."

34.

I slammed the door on my way out of school and ran down the street-over the cement dunes and past the sleepy neighborhoods. I took the back road on my way home to avoid running into anybody. It took me an hour but I still managed to get home before 4.

I sat down outside my house and thought about what to do. Things were supposed to be back in place in my life. Everything should be ok now. But that wasn't true, things were far from ok. I realize now that I am in danger of never being myself again. I let Carter be the center of my life and now that he's gone, my mind is left blank. It's all in my head but I can't move on, I can't see past it.
How can I make this all go away? There is only one thing I can think of.
I walk up to Ida's door and knock loudly three times. She opens after a few beats with a soft smile on her face, gesturing for me to come inside. I shake my head.
"Hey, would you mind dropping me off somewhere? There's something I gotta do real quick." I said, smushing my words together.
Ida eyed me suspiciously, lowering her red frames onto her nose. "What are you up to kid?" Ida grabbed the keys to her car and we both shambled in.
The sun hung lower across the sky, lazily resting its arms across the horizon and sending faint rays of orange hues in through my windshield. Ida lowered the mirror and adjusted in her seat. The cool afternoon air was beginning to set in and made the tiny hairs on my arms stand up. I shivered and turned down the radio.

"So, why are we going here so late?" Ida asked, gesturing to the faint green numbers on the dash and turning to face me in the seat next to her. She smiled halfway.

I shrugged. "It's five o'clock. It's not that late."

"Yeah, I know. But your parents have been pretty strict recently. Thought they barely let you leave the house during the week near dinner."

I turned my face towards the lazy sun. "I don't know. Guess they're letting up."

It was quiet for a while after that so I turned the radio up loud again, letting the sound of the smooth guitar and orange haze keep me contained. I could tell Ida didn't want to pry with me but she knew something was up. We reached the grocery store outside of town about fifteen minutes later. The sun was falling beneath the sky, lower and lower.

"Alright. We're here. You need anything else?" I smiled and pulled my thin sweatshirt over my chest.

"No, I'm good. Thank you for driving." I breathed, smiling darkly, staring at her hands instead of her face. Ida nodded.

"Yeah of course, anytime, you know that." I picked up my bag, looking Ida in the eyes as I did. It was almost eerie the way her eyes shone and bore into me. Unwavering and comforting. Almost begging me to step back in the car.

"What time did you want me to pick you up?" Ida asked, breaking the uncomfortable eye contact. I leaped out of her car and slammed the door, leaning in through the window.

"I don't need a ride home.!" I said using my best fake everything's fine voice. Ida nodded reluctantly, pulling slowly out of the parking lot with a few glances over her shoulder. I watched as she left and sighed heavily, looking across the street.

I ran across and stood under the bus stop sign, sitting at the edge of the bench beside an older man with some plastic bags in his hands. I looked at my phone for the time and then out at the street. A car was pulling up in front of us.

Ida rolled down the window.

"I thought you said you were just getting groceries."

I sighed and scooted further down on the bench.

"I changed my mind."

"Yeah right, kid. Your fake nonchalant voice is dog crap. Where are you really going?"

I eyed her with suspicion. I wanted to trust Ida. I do trust her. She probably already knows.

"The lighthouse?" she suggested bluntly.

I felt a pang of warmth in my heart and nodded. Ida sighed and put her car in park.

"Get in the car."

I crossed my arms, feeling the gaze of the strange man at the other side of the bench.

"Get *in*."

"You're not gonna change my mind, Ida. I *have* to do this." Ida shook her head and leaned through her open window.

"I know you do. But you're not taking a public bus in Alliance by yourself. Get in the car. I'll take you there."

I bit my lip and stood up a little straighter. The bus's closest stop to the park was two and a half miles down the road at a pub. I didn't really want to do that as it was. I walked towards the car, leaning in through the window.

"You promise to take me there?"

"I would never lie to you kid."

I hopped into the car and closed the door with a soft click behind me. I slung the seatbelt across my shoulder and watched as Ida pulled the car out of park and smiled at me. She had been smiling a lot recently.

35.

On our way out of the horrible town that was Alliance, North Carolina, the first place we stopped was at a gas station ten minutes from the bus stop. I was annoyed at first but then I realized I hadn't eaten dinner yet. Ida got her potato chips, and I grabbed a pack of mint gum, a bag of popcorn, and a handful of tropical flavor jolly ranchers.

"What are you doing?"

"What."

"That's the worst flavor."

"I like it."

We hopped back in Ida's car and kept driving. Ida turned out of the gas station and onto the highway.

We rolled down the windows and watched as the town limit for Alliance passed. I felt a sudden feeling of relief pass over me as we did and Ida laughed.

"Bye assholes!" Ida shouted, cackling wildly to herself.

I looked at her incredulously and laughed.

"Ok, well, we're finally out of there. Do we know where we're going?"

"Sort of." I said, reaching for my phone in my pocket. I looked over at Ida and shook my head at her chomping down on a slim jam as she bobbed her head along to Frank Sinatra's greatest hits.

"Get the map out." I looked at her strangely. "Get the map out. It's under your seat."

I reached under my seat and pulled out a map. Crinkled and old and covered in new spidery handwriting. The penciled in notes and locations blurred in with the actual locations, making it even harder to actually read.

"Is this map even accurate?"

"Should be. Land masses don't just move do they?"

I shook my head and unfurled it. "Can't I just use my phone instead?"

"No, that's no fun. Getting lost is part of that old road trip appeal."

"This is not a road trip. This is my attempt at finding closure."

"Potato, tomato."

I shook my head. "Lucky for you, I've never read a map."

"No time like the present, doll."

I bit my lip and squinted at the locations on the map.

"Jesus, why didn't you write this stuff on a separate piece of paper, I can barely read it."

"I thought it would look cool. What's the first thing on there?"

"Thing?"

"Where am I going!"

"Oh. Take, uh, 95. Next exit." I brought the map closer to my face and followed the list up with my finger. A little black dot by the shoreline with the name of the lighthouse under it.

"There she is," Ida pointed as she pulled off. "How far from the border?"

"Border? Don't you mean shoreline?"

"Yeah, whatever."

"It's at the shoreline. It's a lighthouse."

"How far away is it?"

"Probably about a two-and-a-half-hour drive."

"That leaves us just enough time to plan."

"Plan for what?"

"All the shenanary we're gonna do there."

"Shenanary? Well, that's not a word."

"Yes it is I just said it."

"Look, I love you Ida but we're going to do this for Carter, not for ourselves. Let's keep the shenanary to a minimum."

"Fine."

I reached underneath the seat and felt another stack of thickly bound papers.

"What are these?"

"Huh? Oh, more maps."

"Why so many?"

"I like to draw out plans of road trips I wanna take on there."

"Oh, that's cool."

I opened up the maps and my eyes widened. Almost every state was highlighted with a red sharpie.

"You've been to all these places?"

"Nah. They're just dreams. Places I wanna see if I ever get the courage to leave Alliance.'

"Why isn't New York highlighted on any of these?"

"New York?"

"Yeah, I mean, that's where everyone seems to go if they want to figure things out."

"Oh yeah, like who?"

"I don't know, Taylor Swift, Al Capone."

"Oh yeah, and look at the two of them. One a dead money hungry criminal and the other hiding in her million dollar apartment and complaining about how stressed out she is. Why would you use them two as examples?"

"I don't know, New York sounds pretty cool to me."

"Honey, New York sounds cool to everybody, and that just makes it more disappointing up close. New York is full of assholes. You can't even see the sky with all that smog and poverty hanging in the air."

"Woah, didn't realize you hated New York."

"I lived there for three months and got spat back out by the Statue of Liberty herself."

"Seems about right."

--

We drove with light traffic because it was Monday and the sun was going down. The old morning. The light blue walls giving way to the stardust. The delicate pull of the night collecting the sky in its fingers, mixing the orange with the black on its small and tender pinky, creating feelings in inanimate objects.

The night felt gentle and meek as we continued on down the road. I could feel my anger mellow out slightly as we drove further away from Alliance and into the dark night. The moon smiled through the sheer curtain clouds and danced lazily across our bodies and heaps of junk scattered around the car. It was getting later and the crickets were just beginning to replace the birds.

Tall trees the color of dust began to spring up as we drove along the coast. Thin and whimpering with the wind and mountain air.

"Look," Ida exclaimed, pointing to a faded blue sign by the road.

"Hey."

"Get out the map. I got a feeling I gotta get off soon."

I opened up the map, following the route with my finger again.

"Nope. Stay on this for another thirty miles or so."

"Damn it. My senses aren't as sharp as they used to be."

I put the map back down on my lap and rested my head against the back of my seat, listening to the sound of the wind through my slightly cracked window.

I thought about him.

We got to the lighthouse around 8:45 to discover that the so-called park that surrounds it does not mean a collection of sad swings and a slide by a water fountain, but a huge army of trees and ponds in the middle of a forest. The top of the lighthouse could be seen just beyond the trees just about a mile in through the trail.

"Alright, well. I don't get out much. Let me put my traveling shoes on."

Ida popped open her trunk and grabbed a pair of steel-toed boots from the bottom of her suitcase.

"Why do you have those?"

"I used to work in construction."

"Oh. I didn't know that."

"Well, now you do. What shoes are you wearing darling?"

"These," I gestured to my white sneakers and smiled.

Ida looked down at my feet and grimaced. "What else you got."

"These are it."

"What are you twelve?"

"They're comfy. Besides, there's a trail you know."

"Well ok then."

I pulled on the heel of my sneakers and eyed Ida from under my lashes, already beginning to take off her slip ons and throw them into the trunk. I bit my lip guiltily. "You don't need to come with me you know."

Ida paused and let the boots she was holding fall to her side. "You think I'm gonna wait in the car for you for three hours? I don't think so."

"I saw a pub or something near the entrance of the park. You can go there if you want. I won't stay long."

"That's alright kid. I'm fine right here."

I grimaced and folded my arms across my chest. "I really appreciate you taking me up here Ida. But I kinda want to do this part on my own."

Ida stared at me hard, searching my face with her eyes. I wanted to be alone. I accepted that Ida was coming initially but as I got closer, the pain in my chest felt tighter.

"Well, if that's what you want kid. You know I'll never turn down a cold glass of Budweiser."

I nodded and turned towards the path. "Hey, wait." I looked back at Ida's form through the darkness. "Call me if you need me. I'll come running."

I nodded again and turned back towards the stairs, slinging my bookbag over my shoulder and climbing the steps towards the lighthouse. And I didn't look back. Not even once. It was different for me to act so nonchalant. To leave without a real goodbye.

36.

The words from Carter's journal whispered in my ear as I followed the ill-lit trail towards the lighthouse. It felt weird being there, like I had already seen it before. But I only knew it from words. On a normal day, I would have been easily spooked by the dark woods surrounding me. But today, I didn't really care at all. I walked for little more than fifteen minutes when I saw a break in the path ahead.

I felt my hair begin to be whipped across my face as I exited the path in the woods. It was a dark and windy night, the only lights coming from the dim lamps across the paths and the light from the lighthouse occasionally shining down at me. I ran my hands up and down my arms, trying to contain the warmth that was left in me.

I stared up at it. The lighthouse. It was a tall and menacing looking structure, painted with the darkest black and the whitest white I'd ever seen. Some parts of it were rusty and stale but most of it was still intact. I stalked slowly around it in a circle, taking it all in with an awed expression. It wasn't that great of a building, but it felt somehow like the most magnificent thing I'd ever seen.

I let my eyes follow the pattern of the huge light guiding people out at sea. It was bright and slow and almost beckoned me to walk up to find it. I lowered my eyes slowly from the top of the structure down towards its base. I walked towards the wooden door by the base, feeling the anticipation grow rapidly inside me with each step. I came up to the door and put my hand on the knob, turning it slightly to the left. Then the right. I pulled the knob towards me, leaning back on my heels with all my body weight. Nothing. I pushed the door in, digging my feet into the gravel. I pushed and felt the panic start to rise in my chest as my arms turned red from the strain. It was locked.

I felt my breath quicken and the anger rise within me again. Are you fucking serious? How could I be so stupid? Of course it's closed it's almost ten o' clock. I grabbed my head in my hands and looked around at my surroundings for a clue of what to do. At the base of the lighthouse sat a small collection of rocks. Perfect. I picked up a particularly heavy and jagged piece. I walked a few feet away from the door and turned again to face it, swinging my arm back and hurling it forward with everything I had.

The glass didn't break and the rock bounced off, landing only a little bit in front of me.

I stared back at the rock and the door, approaching it again and turning the door, pounding on the door, and yelling up at the light.

Nothing. Nobody. Stupid.

You should be here. You should be feeling what I feel. Telling me to calm down and stop getting so frustrated. The air is cold but the breeze is warm. It's perfect except it's horrible.

Where are you?

The wind was angry for you. She whipped my thick brown hair in my face.

I moved my eyes off the lighthouse and out to the ocean. The shoreline was over there, I could just barely see it out by there. I walked slowly over. A huge basin was revealed beneath my feet and the sand I stood upon. I walked until my toes touched the very edge and wiped the sweat off my forehead, despite the chill that was developing in my thin sweatshirt.

The black shimmering silk reflected back at me the colors of the night like a watercolor painting. Electric blue tendons from distant lights shot out across the black, enveloping the shadowy figures of boats that sat delicately atop the surface. A red fire from the edge of the tide to the middle of the bridge, ebbing and flowing gently. I stood there staring, letting the cool breeze dance across my bare knees and old t-shirt. I rubbed my foot gently across my shivering leg, biting my lip at the painting ahead. The gentle sway of the black evening covering the sun like a dark sheet.

I breathed slowly. In for five. Hold for three. Out for eight. Over and over. My heart was beating wildly from the memories and the tall moon. It was cold. I could really feel it this time.

My backpack dug deep into my shoulder blades and my breathing was uneven. I stood looking out at the bitter water, looking past the black and trying to let the beauty of it all in the morning take me in too. Take me back into the colors of the sunsets and the leaves from the trees. Things I grew up knowing and loving. I dug my boots into the soil and opened my arms, closing my eyes. Take me back. I thought. *Take me back.* I felt so disconnected.

I hadn't realized until then that it wasn't just people I had shut out. It was my own life, my own love, and interests. My own self.

"Come on. Come on." I whispered, my brow furrowing. Suddenly I felt a voice call out towards me. I opened my eyes, but it wasn't you. It was her.

"You can't do it."

I turned my head slightly from the black water and saw Ida there. She was out of breath and had a concerned look on her face. Why did she have to follow me everywhere?

I felt my chest tighten more and more as she stepped closer.

"Please go back. Leave me alone." I said as I backed up into the water, the cold waves biting bitterly at my heels.

"No. You can't do it."

"What are you talking about?"

"You can't push me away, Dyl. *This* is your life! *This* is what you got. I know it seems horrible but-"

"Oh, some god damn *life* this is! What fun! I get to spend my days reliving nightmare after nightmare, a never-ending cycle of bullshit! I can't stand another second of it Ida! My happiness died out in August, the only thing that's left is pain and failure."

"That's not true and you know it."

"Please stop."

I let my arms fall to my sides and opened my eyes. Ida came to stand beside me, looking out across the water.

"Sure is a pretty view, huh?"

I shook my head.

"What exactly were you planning on doing out here anyway?"

I shrugged. "Go into the lighthouse. See what he wanted to see. Have one last great adventure."

"Our road trip here was fun. Isn't that adventure enough?"

"It wasn't just the lighthouse. It was the feeling it was supposed to give me. A sign or something."

"A sign. And what was this sign supposed to say?"

"Anything. A cue for me to start my life over again, to move on."

Ida shook her head.

"No one gets a sign, Dylan. It takes time."

"It's been months. Months of nothing but pain."

"Not every day. Some days I saw you smile."

"They were never real."

"Some of them were. Maybe you just didn't know it."

"I'm telling you that's not true because it's gone."

"What's gone?"

"My love for this life. My reason to go on. I can't find it anymore."

"Don't say that kid, things will get better. I know things seem bad right now but he's just one boy-"

"Stop. Please stop. It's not just him. It's me, you, everything. I don't want to be here anymore."

"We can leave whenever you want Dylan."

"It's not the lighthouse Ida, Jesus. I don't wanna be *here*. I don't wanna be in this world. On this Earth. It doesn't want me anymore."

Ida furrowed her brow and shook her head. Her mouth moved slowly like she wanted to say something. She walked slowly towards me, kicking up sand with her boots until I could feel her hot and shaky breath on my face. There was a tremor in her voice. She spoke quietly yet with more anger than I'd ever heard in a person's voice.

"Don't ever say that to me. Not ever again."

I shook my head and bit my lip. I took a breath and felt the wind rack my body and instill the cold into my bones. The colors of the moon sank into my vision and I slowly sat down upon the cold and withered sand.

"He's not here like he promised, Ida. I don't feel him, I should feel him. I'm so alone now. Even his imaginary self has left me. I'm so alone now, so fucking depressed. Every day is another field of smoke and ruin that I have to stumble through."

"That's not true kid, you know he's here. You know you're not alone in this."

I frowned deeper, letting the tears drown my face and the water pull me in, drown in me.

"Do I?"

A silence. A quiet apology from the waves as they brushed against me. A mournful sigh from the leaves as they feel down from the trees and got sucked into the black night.

"Ida, what if it wasn't just Carter that died? What if it was me too."

"Oh please, what the hell are you-"

"Just listen. When Carter died, I thought I'd never be ok. I believed I would forever be stuck wallowing in pain. About a month after he died his brother came to my house with the notebook. His notebook. I read it over and over again. I thought about it all the time. The things we hadn't done that we should have, the things unsaid, the time, the life wasted. I thought that the notebook would be closure for me but it wasn't. It just made things worse. That was when I realized how badly I was hurt by his death. He was more than a friend to me, he was- is a part of me. I feel as if I can never recover. I'll never be myself again."

"Kid, please understand what I'm about to you say to you, ok? Listen, you're hurt, of course you are. Anyone would be, I felt your pain once too. I still feel it sometimes. It's ok to feel the way you do, but you can't let the pain defeat you. I told you about my husband. About how I didn't leave the house until I absolutely had to. What I didn't tell you is that after he died, I lost 30 pounds. I didn't eat anything. Everything tasted like sandpaper. I could barely walk. I thought I was going to die that way, starving myself to death out of grief."

I looked at Ida sadly with my eyes as she continued.

"You wanna know who saved me? You did. You were so young I bet you don't remember. I passed out in the front yard getting the mail and you saw me lying there, got your mama to come help me. If it were not for you Dylan, I have no doubt in my mind that I would be dead right now."

I sucked in air through my teeth and grabbed her gently by the shoulder to steady myself against the harsh wind. I thought hard and tried to remember. "Are you telling the truth?"

"Of course I am kid. I would never lie about something so pathetic." I looked back out at the ocean as Ida moved to sit closer to me.

"So now I'm returning the favor. I'm trying to save you from yourself right now and let you know that life is worth living. It absolutely is. I need you to know from the bottom of my heart that you are not alone. Ever. There is always someone there. Sometimes even more than just one person."

"What about the other people? The people that make life harder."

"Forget them! They don't know, it's not about them. Stick around for the people that love you, like me. Like your mom, your dad. I'm here for you. I wasn't obligated to drive you here but when I saw you here looking so angry at the world, I came here with you. Why do you think I did that?"

"I don't know."

"Because I care about you. Because despite your pain and constantly pushing me away I love you. *I'm* here for you, Dylan. I want you to be happy again. You're so young, you've got so much life left to live. I know why you came here tonight. But you can't do it."

"Why shouldn't I? No one would care that I'm gone. Not even me. The only person that did isn't here anymore."

"You're wrong. You've got me. You've got Martha. Sure, she drinks. But that's only because she's guilty for feeling like a bad mom. You have your dad that wants to get close to you but doesn't know how. You've got your brother, Sawyer, Carlos. You have Peter and me and, you know what, you still have Carter. You can't let that bully inside you take over yourself. Because right now, your own mind is the biggest enemy of all. It's your grief that's killing you, not other people. You've touched so many people in life, Dyl. Please, don't give up yet. Carter seemed to love this life, I wish you would too." I dug my feet see beneath the sand- in between my toes. I let Ida's words wash over me and settle into the pit in my stomach.

I looked at Ida. It would take more than words to cure this pain. "I wanna love this life."

I looked out at the water and dropped my bag on the ground. I grabbed her hand and led her into the water. She slowly followed beside me. We walked until we were just below the waist. I looked at her again and told her a short story about a boy that hated the ocean but wanted to love it since he lived so close. I laid on my back and let the wind blow.

I floated there and waited for the waves to drown me. I let the ocean surround me and drained my salty tears in with the sea. The storm was rough yet oddly gentle as it rocked me back and forth. I choked on my tears and the foam. I shut my eyes and laid and tried to love the ocean. And then I say there thinking. Thinking about that night that I hadn't thought about since it happened. Some things I hope I never remember. It's too difficult to think that I was once a part of something so cruel. Something so raw and full of potential that was brutally crushed behind the wheel of an old and broken car. The day it happened was relentless.

37.
August 26th, 2017

There's an exception to every rule. The crosswalks that are mere suggestions, the turning signals that don't really seem to do anything. He drives- he *drove* a 2001 sand-colored Toyota Camry with duct tape on the driver's side window. One of those generic old little four doors with the windows that crank and the paint that's scratched and peeling.

This unreliable piece of junk is one of those oxymoron types. It's ugly but it's beautiful. It's one of the few objects in my memories with him that is fond and recurring.

It's taken me a long time to have the courage to revisit this chapter. The chapter that brought about the sickness and the pain and, eventually, the death. Some days were good days. Some days were sunshine and pizza days, spending time with old friends and laughing at the ceiling as we wiggled our toes. Those are the ones that are hardest to remember.

8 PM. A lazy Saturday night. We got matching t-shirts at the Stop and Shop with a dragon on it. Just for fun. The kind of stupid stuff you only do with someone when you're in love.

The sun shone through a small crack in the trees followed behind me as I peered in wonder over the side of a cliff and gasped. My fingers grasped onto the edge of your t-shirt and you laughed at me, throwing your head back with delight.

"You have the emergency brake on, right?"

"Don't worry, Jenny's not going anywhere."

We were at a new place an hour away from home. A small observatory on the side of a cliff in New Milford.

We pulled into the parking lot just after night fell. The place opened at 9 so we sat in the car for a little while eating pretzels and staring straight off of a steep cliff, talking about how we never wanted to turn back.

At 8:50 you and I opened up the doors of the car and headed towards the big round structure. It was unsuspecting and old looking. When you opened up the door there was a little museum and meeting room where you first walked in. We walked up a short flight of stairs and into a large dome-shaped room where the telescope was constructed.

"Says here it's the original telescope. Second largest in the world." you marveled, reading the back of a pamphlet you grabbed on the way in.

"Too cheap to take me to the first largest?" I joked, kicking the back of your heels softly as we walked slowly around the small dome. You and I were the only people there besides a cute Asian couple and the tour guide. Small doors on the roof opened to reveal the sky above. It was a beautiful night to look up at the sky. A brilliant and big moon with clear skies and bright stars. The tour guide hopped on a tall ladder, using a rope to propel around the floor.

"Getting to the nearest star would be a 75,000-year journey." the tour guide continued as we looked up at the open roof.
The tour guide used a small knob to lower the scope and gestured for one of us to try it out. He let me go first. I climbed up the ladder and leaned back, guiding my eye up to the small lens. I let it focus and I gasped, letting the sight of space take over me. I stood looking up at it all while the tour guide kept talking about it. I didn't really care how it all worked in that moment. All I knew was that I was staring at one of the most beautiful things I've ever seen.
I took my eye off the lens after a while and looked down at you. You were smiling up too. But not at the sky, at me. A lazy kind of smile that was so comforting to me. I stepped down and you raised your eyebrows at me.

"Cool?" you whispered to me. "See for yourself." I said as you ascended the ladder. I watched as you brought the lens to your face and smiled widely. I smiled at your smile that I loved so much. After a minute you came back down again and we let the others all take a turn. We didn't spend more of an hour there when we each decided to walk outside by the cliff. There was a small picnic bench there and a terrace that overlooked the cliff. There were lanterns set up out there as well as a few other forms of lighting. I pulled my sweatshirt on over my head as the wind raked across my body and the cool night air sent small chills down my spine.

I looked out at the chasm below us as I leaned over the railing. I looked back at you and you were looking at me again. You with your dragon t-shirt and dark jeans.

I looked at you with a playful suspicion and walked slyly towards you.

"Why do you keep staring at me playboy?"

"I'm not staring. I'm admiring." I rolled my eyes.

"Easy there kid, I don't think you can handle all this." I quipped, gesturing to myself and making a weird face.

You laughed softly and walked towards me.

"You like this place?" you asked.

"Yeah, it's really cool. How'd you find it?"

You shrugged. "Just luck. I wanted to find someplace that was special."

"Special? And how do you categorize a place that's special."

"I don't know. A beautiful place. A place that people would die to see." you put your arms over my chest and rested your chin on my forehead. We stared out across the black and the night.

"Why are you acting so weird?" I asked suddenly.

"It's beautiful here, isn't it?"

"Stop talking about how beautiful everything is. Come on, what are you thinking?"

"Can I talk about how beautiful *someone* is?" I stepped away from you as you released your grip on me.

"What?" I said, feeling the blood rush into my cheeks.

"You're beautiful."

"Stop saying beautiful so much."

You looked down at your feet. "If I ask you a question, do you promise to give me a truthful answer?"

I looked over at you suspiciously. "Yeah, of course."

You fiddled awkwardly with your hands. Almost like that first day you met me. We were both so young and nervous.

You took a small step toward me and looked me seriously in the eyes. "Do you love me?"

Love. So many things come stumbling off that word. So many fucking things. It's intrusive, it's selfish if you're not careful. I've never really been one for careful in the first place so that word just makes it all worse.

"Do I love you?" I asked slowly, letting the words fall gently across my tongue.

"Yeah."

"What do you mean?"

"Me. You. Not like friends but together."

I laughed at you. "Well, I don't think I know yet."

"Why not?"

I looked down at my feet as I felt you walk closer.

"You've known me for ten years. Why would you wait until we only have one year left together to tell me this?"

He shrugged. "I wanted to find the perfect place and the perfect time."

"Those things don't exist, Carter. It's never gonna be perfect."

"I know. And I didn't realize that until recently. That's what took me so long."

I looked up at you as you looked at me questioningly.

"So, what's the answer?"

I licked my lips and felt the weight in my chest get a little heavier. "I wanna love you."

"Oh yeah?"

"Yeah."

"And what's stopping you?"

"I'm afraid of losing you."

"Don't be."

I leaned in towards your face and closed my eyes, gripping your dragon shirt in my palm and letting the smell of your cologne fill my senses.

And my best friend Carter Higgins kissed me. The first kiss I'd ever had. Surrounded by pretty little lanterns in a beautiful place that we drove an hour to see. Just you and me and the stars and a steep cliff, a dark and windy night full of genuine smiles. I guess you could say it was a perfect night.

And then the clouds came.

--

We talked about how sorry we were to have waited to tell each other things and then eventually how tired we were. We marveled at the arrival of some heavy and sudden rain and decided to leave before the car fell off the cliff. It started with the rain. The beginning of the end of the night. We piled into the old car and you started it, warily stepping on the emergency brake and backing out of the parking lot to the road. You were smiling wide and our adrenaline was high.

"LUCY IN THE SKY-Y WITH DI-A-MONDS!" Heads slamming on the broken in headrests, arms flailing wildly, voices straining to match the voice coming from the radio. You know who.

Your hand brushed against the volume as we stopped at a light. I sighed.

"What'd you do that for!"

you smiled, the car bathed in a dusty red light. "I just wanted to say something I didn't get a chance to when we were on the balcony."

I sat up in the chair and leaned toward him. "Oh yeah, what more could you possibly say in one night?'

"I just wanted to say I'm sorry for not telling you sooner. I hope I didn't say anything too late."

"Carter. You're barely eighteen, I'm still seventeen. We barely know anything about life let alone love. We have years left of our lives to learn about those things. One of the few things I do know about anything is that I absolutely love spending time with you. And a little bit of college is not gonna to change that."

"Well good. Cause I got a lot more planned for us in the future." I laughed a happy laugh and sat back in my chair, nodding and rubbing my eyes as you continued to talk and the rain continued to fall. The sound of the quiet radio switched to the voice of another man as the light switched green. You hummed along to the tune and I watched the cars pass by.

It's weird how different things look at night. The cars turn from metal shopping carts to spaceships with the flip of a light switch. The hazy glow of the moon and the lights from the cars made my eyes twinkle. I smile at his soft humming and the bumpy road and close my eyes. It's always the bumpiest rides that are the most memorable. I joined in for the harmony and wiggled my eyebrows to the beat, tapping my foot and really feeling it all.

"I like this song." I chimed, my hand nudging the knob along till the music became part of the night. We stopped humming and sang at the top of our lungs again, the car struggling along, the lights passing and the clock reading 11:03. 11:03. We were close to home. We were close.

The first thing I remember was seeing the headlights flash brightly, blinding me of the trees and the road and everything that surrounded me. I heard a shout and a pair of lights flashing and a force that felt like getting punched in the gut. Machine on machine, crashing into each other in a harsh crunch of metal pieces. A sound like a sonic boom forcing my eyes shut. The people inside disregarded like rag dolls. Gravity gone, my air knocked out of me, choking on my own shock and confusion. The sounds somehow stopped except for a shrill high-pitched ringing noise. Spinning and rolling and pain. I could see every moment like it was happening forever. My muscles were tense as I fumbled wildly for something to hold my body down to the seat. I remember screaming and slamming on breaks and that everything felt loud. But then it was silent. Nothing was working. It all happened in five seconds, but the sheer force of the impact was enough to shake my life forever.

--

My ears were ringing and my body felt numb. The lack of colors was mixed in with the sour taste of salt, blood, and mango lip gloss. I struggled to open my eyes, I felt my body contorted in a weird position like I was close to falling but being held up by something jagged and rough. I heard voices in the distance but none of them sounded familiar. I felt exhausted and hot among the heavy rain and wind. I could barely feel my face. I mumbled softly, my throat felt like sandpaper and I could taste blood.

"Carter." I begged. "Carter." Your name fell out like a whisper but I said it over and over. I blinked and squinted my eyes. The windshield was cracked and some parts of it were missing. I turned my head and winced, fumbling around to find my seatbelt. It was dark, the only source of light coming from the street lamp around the bend in the road. I finally heard a click as the seat belt released and fell back slowly.

I grimaced as I tried to push myself out of my seat, I leaned over slightly to look at the driver's side. You weren't in your seat. The driver's window was smashed and your part of the front windshield was completely destroyed. I felt a sort of lump rise up in my throat at the possibility of him walking away from his car. I struggled to open the door but finally did with a weak push.

I shuffled out of my seat beside the highway. The sky was a cool grey. I felt that color wallowing deep within my stomach. Damp hair stuck to my sweaty and rain drenched cheeks. My hands shook in my sweatshirt. My lids fell lower and my feet were numb. Numb from the cold, the sounds, the everything. I glanced up at the car that had hit us, it was making a beeping sound. The front of the car was completely smashed. I didn't hear anyone inside of it.

I could barely move or see. My sweatshirt covered half my damp hair, but the exposed ones hang down limply in front of my eyes, shielding me from the sight of the car. The trees around me were dead. So dead. The grass broke apart easily with each pitiful shuffle I made as I circled around from my side of the car to yours. The mud caked up all around my knees and shins. The only thing that reminded me that I was not that tree, that I was not dead or dying or forgotten was my warm and tremulous breath huffing out of my chapped and cold lips.

A lady in a Subaru was pulled over gesturing wildly to our car while she was on the phone. She looked at me with a look of surprise and asked if I was ok. I ignored her as I stepped to the back of the car, holding onto the Camry for support. The cars were next to the highway in a grassy ditch. A few cars flew by us but this road was mostly quiet. As I rounded to your side of the car, I saw something laying down a few feet away from the car off the side. I stumbled over to it.

I leaned down, using my hands to support me against the cool ground. And then I saw that it was not something laying there, it was you. Bloody and unmoving. I grabbed your face and breathed your name over and over, yelling at that lady to call an ambulance, holding you against me and crying despite the pain in my chest and the feeling of your blood on my skin. I did everything I could. I don't want to think about it anymore.

I almost died to tell you the truth. On a perfect night in August.

38.

<u>Present</u>

I can't think anymore. I blocked that out long ago. I hadn't thought of it a day since it happened. I thought I was saving myself the pain, but maybe that's what's been causing it all along.

But it kick-started something inside me and all at once I felt it. The trees, the air, the wind, the laugh. Tumbling out like my next breath. What a feeling, to be completely overwhelmed and to be completely over life at the same time. My first breath since eight months ago that I actually felt I should be taking. Like I was worth the small path of nothing that waited for me. Everything aligning and feeling right. That's a feeling you don't know you have until you really know. A gut feeling I think it's called.

I lifted my head up at the water and saw Ida looking at me. She was smiling a genuine smile. I stood up in the water and walked over to her, hugging her with all I had left within me.

"I'm ready to go." I stammered as I pulled away.

Ida looked slightly concerned. "Where do you want to go?" I shook my head and smiled.

"Home."

So we got in the car and turned on the radio. The street lamps on the side of the road guided us towards our final stop. And as we passed by the trees and the buildings and everything that was North Carolina, I got to thinking about my life up until that point. Those silver people that I loved and knew that were not immortal. Like the one that keeps turning the radio up really loud next to me. Or the ones back home with real issues regarding empathy. And me. And Carter.

Going to that lighthouse was not something I wanted to do. It was something I needed to do. When we left I felt hopeful. When we got here I felt scared. When the door wouldn't open I felt angry. And when I laid down in that water, I felt everything. I thought about that night that I shut out of my brain and I accepted that it really did happen. Not just the bad parts though, also the good parts. The happy parts. And I think in that strange way I think I found closure or something. I just didn't realize that that ability to forgive myself and the world was within me all along. You find it in yourself with time. Time changes things, it changes people. It changed me. People help too. Like Ida and my mom, dad and Sam, Sawyer and Carlos, Pete, TJ. Everyone helps.

39.
February 13, 2018

I didn't lie to my family about where I was or what I was doing out past one in the morning. They sat and listened quietly, my mom shaking her head sometimes like she knew it all along. I told them about the notebook, about TJ, even about myself. It's weird to think that I hadn't really done that much before. I told them that above all else, I had found the closure that I needed in the form of an old lighthouse 40 miles up the coast that I had never seen before. They didn't ask about my damp shorts or stiff hair.

After I talked they sat silent for a moment. Then they each got up and hugged me and told me they loved me, that they were glad I was ok. If you told me that is how they'd react 3 months ago, I would have laughed at you. With only a few months left of school, they told me to stay home and finish the year with them.

The next day I wake up late but with a mission in my head. I groggily got out of bed and changed into a jean skirt, a black shirt, and my purple hat. I pulled the covers up on my bed and tucked the notebook into my bag.

I swung my leg over my bike and pedaled slowly, feeling the wind rush past my ears and run all over my face like soft kisses. I stopped in front of the Stop and Shop and went inside for a minute, grabbing a bouquet of bright yellow flowers and laying them in the bag with his notebook. went out past the park in the center of town, past Oja's coffee, and just past the docks to a wide-open field with gray monuments. The cemetery.

I laid my bike against the first tree I saw and walked in through the headstones. I didn't go to the funeral, didn't think I had it in me. I beat myself up for not going after. I figure I can make up for something lost maybe now.

His was three steps back behind a big tree with tall branches to the middle left of the field. Carter Morris Higgins. April 12th 2001-August 24th 2017. And that was that. Someone's whole life summed up on the front of a piece of granite with a name and a date. I laid my bag softly on the ground and sat down in front of the headstone. I closed my eyes and tried to slow my breathing, letting the sound of the bluebirds and swaying leaves drown out the sadness I felt flooding into me.

Opening my eyes I reached into my bag, pulling out the bouquet of yellow flowers and smelling them softly, letting the cold make my cheeks turn pink a little bit.

"Well, I know how much you love spontaneous gifts so, I got you these," I confessed, laying the flowers softly in front of him. "Don't know what kind you like, guys don't really tell you their favorite flower much nowadays."
I traced the letters of his name with my eyes, wondering if by some miracle he would suddenly appear in front of me.

"Um, I don't really know how to say any of this. But, I miss you. Really bad. It's literally driving me crazy, I mean I literally think I see you sometimes still."
I looked around the cemetery at the other headstones and the few people. Some were crying, some were talking. I'm glad I wasn't the only one hoping.

"I'm sorry I didn't go to your funeral. I just didn't think I could do it. It just felt so fast. It's like, three days after you leave the earth they want to put you in the ground." I jiggled my foot and brought my legs in together, pulling my hat off my head and laying it on top of my bag.

"I felt bitter and angry that you were...dead. You are dead. That some absolute *idiot* killed you because he was on his phone. What a useless way for someone so completely incredible to go."
I looked up at the sky as I felt some lone tears roll down my cheeks and fall into the grass.

"You deserve so much better. You're just so smart and so beautiful and the best person I've ever met. And this-this is how the world treats you," I gestured to his gravestone in aggravation.
I shook my head and bit my lip, trying to contain myself.

"But it happened. And I can't change that. No matter how much I wish I could."
I lowered my eyes into my lap and picked at a few blades of grass. I reached for my bag and moved my hat aside, pulling out Carter's notebook and touching the cover fondly.

"Anyways, I'm not here to tell you I'm angry because I'm sure you are too. I got your notebook," I said pulling it out and holding it up. "From TJ. He said you'd want me to have that and I hope that's true because I read all of it. Every word that you've written in here since you were seven."
I put the notebook back down and unraveled the twine that held it together. I opened it up and flipped through the pages, letting individual words stand out to me and force me to smile at your handwriting.

"It's amazing. And without this notebook, I don't think I would be sitting here today with you." I babbled, flipping the book closed and staring again at the headstone.

"I know you kept this because it helped you save yourself, but I can't help but feel like this is the only thing that saved me."

"I guess I just want to say thank you. Thank you for the last ten years of my life, which have been unforgettable and so amazing. Even the bad parts have been good because of you. Thank you for constantly making me smile, even when you didn't want to. Thank you for this." I proceeded, gesturing to the notebook. "I miss the days spent skipping school because we could, running down to the dock with our feet in the water, our trips to Taco Bell. Our road trips. God, I miss those." I lamented.

"Above everything else, I miss you. More than I've ever missed anybody else in the world. You were my best friend and you always will be. And I know you're watching over me far above with a smirk on your face. You have to be. Because I feel you everywhere I go. And I love that feeling. And I love you. I don't think I ever really told you that, but I always thought it. I love you."

I sat up on my knees and leaned over the flowers, letting my palm rest against your last name and pressing my forehead against your name. "God, I love you." I whispered.

I sat talking for almost an hour, then I decided I should come back some other day. My eyes lingered on your name as I turned to leave and I promised myself I'd be back real soon.

My mission was not over. Before I left I made a phone call, looking at your name every second as I talked.

Finally, I pulled my hat over my head, picked up my bag, and headed towards my bike, stealing a glance over my shoulder as I left. I went out past the docks and past Oja's coffee shop and through the trail in the woods towards O'Malley's. I leaned my bike against my wall and went inside.

Sawyer was working again but there were only about two tables worth of people there. She smiled at me and we talked.

I sat in a corner booth by the window and just got a water. I sat and waited, looking down at my phone for a call to cancel. But none came. Instead, I felt a finger tap on my shoulder. I looked up and saw Carter's mom. She looked similar to when I last saw her a couple of days after the accident. Tired and stern but strong and somehow welcoming. I stood up from the booth intending to hug her but she just sat down across from me.

It occurred to me a few days ago that, after the accident, I hadn't talked much to Carter's mom. She was always a bit of an outside character in my life. Always working to support her two boys at home. I only ever seemed to see her when Carter and I got into trouble. I think she's always associated me with danger in that way. I was unsure of what to say but I knew I had something to say to her.

"Hi." I greeted, smiling softly at her.

"Hey Dylan." she rasped with a half sort of smile on her face.

"Thank you for meeting me."

She nodded and set her purse down slowly on the booth seat.

"I have to admit I was surprised to have you call me. It's been a long time."

"Yes, yes it has been." I admitted, stealing glances at her from under my eyelashes.

Sawyer came over with my water and Mrs. Higgins ordered a coffee. I stared at her and waited for her reply. Not really sure of where we stood.

"Well. Why'd you call me? Now, after all these months."

I swallowed and adjusted in my seat. "I wanted to call. I did. But I didn't know what to say. I didn't even know where we stood. I meant to come see you after things had died down a bit but things never really did. And it wasn't until now that I thought I felt, maybe, we'd both be ready."

Mrs. Higgins nodded at Sawyer as she sat down her cup of coffee. We both denied wanting anything but a side. I watched as Sawyer left and Mrs. Higgins sipped her coffee. I looked out the window and wondered why I had brought her here in the first place.

"Well," she pondered slowly. "Tell you the truth Dylan, I don't think we'll ever be ready."

I nodded. "Yeah. Maybe you're right." We stared at each other awkwardly for a minute, wondering how long it had been since we last talked.

I cleared my throat and shuffled in my seat. "Um, so, how are you doing?"

Mrs. Higgins laughed softly. "Really?"

I shrugged sheepishly.

"You know when most people ask me that, I roll my eyes and I tell them to leave me alone. But for you, I'll indulge. Mostly because I have questions of my own."

"Ok."

"The last few months have been the worst days of my life. The week of his death I spent just staring at the door of his room. I couldn't even go inside. That was next week's challenge."

She stirred her coffee slowly with her spoon as she talked.

"It took almost three months to just get out of that phase of intense pain and anger and depression. I didn't want to see anyone, I didn't even leave my house except for the funeral."

I averted my eyes as she said that.

"As the months wore on and I realized that the world kept spinning despite the death of my son, I decided to go back to work. And, you know what, that helped a little. It was a nice numbing distraction. And as I worked and left the house a little more, things have gotten just a little easier every day. And things continue to feel easier. But still the sadness lingers and it's everywhere I look."

I looked up at Mrs. Higgins and we made eye contact. It was only then that I recognized the look in her eyes. It was something that I saw in my own eyes too. It was the look of someone who was in pain. She stayed quietly staring so I assumed it was time to respond.

"I can't imagine the feeling of losing a son. I mean I'm only seventeen, but I can imagine the pain of losing a best friend. And it's horrible."

She nodded. "I know that you and I never really talked very much. But I could tell that you and Carter shared something special. You're all he ever seemed to talk about."

I nodded and bit my lip. "Look, Mrs. Higgins, I know I haven't really been there for you since Carter passed away. I was too afraid, even to attend the funeral of my own best friend. But I want you to know that I am here for you now. Because I feel some part of your pain too and I know it hurts. But I also know that you shouldn't deal with it alone. It's better to have people around you. And I hope it's not too late to say that."

Mrs. Higgins looked at me then. Really looked at me. It was almost like seeing TJ the day he gave me the notebook. She reached across the table and took my hand and smiled a genuine smile.

"It's not too late. In fact, if you had told me that a few months ago I would have probably strangled you out of anger. But now I feel ready to lean on others. And I really would love to know more about who Carter was to you. And I'd love to share who Carter was to me with you."

"I'd like that very much."

I released her hand gently and reached into my bag, pulling out the notebook. "But you don't have to hear it from me. You can hear it from him." I said as I handed her the notebook. I felt the weight of its pages lifting off my fingers and I sunk down deeper into my chair.

"What's this?"

"It's Carter's journal. TJ gave it to me a little while ago. I figured he hadn't told you. I know you two have had a rocky relationship."

She unraveled the twine and began to flip open to the first page, reading the first words and smiling. And then crying. She put her hand over her mouth and then softly shut the book, her fingers lingering over the cover.

"I didn't think he would actually start one."

I nodded and watched as she put the notebook back on top of her bag.

"Thank you."

"I shouldn't have kept it in the first place."

"No. I'm glad you did. He would have wanted you to read it."

I smiled. "There's something you should know about TJ. You can find it in the journal if you want or I can tell you now. It's about his arrest."

Mrs. Higgins looked up at me with teary eyes. "TJ's arrest? Oh, you must not know. A boy came by the house the other day, Peter was his name. I'd never seen him before in my life but he insisted that he needed to talk to TJ about something. He confessed to us that that boy Brady that bullied you and Carter years ago framed TJ. He went to the cops and they both were arrested. TJ's gonna have a clean record now." I smiled out the window as she talked, feeling my smile waver a bit near the end.

"Oh. So he's in jail now?"

Mrs. Higgins nodded. "Yup. I felt a little bad for him. He felt guilty, ashamed. But he said he knew that confessing would mean jail time. He told me that while we were talking. I requested to the officers that Peter be let off a little easier. We'll see what happens."

I nodded. "And where's TJ now?"

"He's at home. I felt so bad about not believing him, I must have apologized a thousand times. But he didn't seem to be so mad, just glad that the truth is finally out."

"Why didn't he tell anyone he was innocent?"

"He said he felt guilty. He didn't want Carter to know he'd been hanging with out with a bully. It was his car, he had no proof, everything seemed to be against him. So he took the time and left."

I nodded and asked more questions. I didn't feel like I had to tell Mrs. Higgins about Peter. She knew enough. I was just glad someone finally took my advice for once.

We talked for hours, swapping stories of Carter and reading some of the ones he had written himself. It was nice. I hadn't realized how much Carter was like his mom.

I hopped on my bike a little before dinner and went home, content with the way things were turning out today. I turned onto the side street past Rosie's Roller Rink and Alliance High, looking up at the trees surrounding the road and dodging little cracks that popped up in front of my tires.

I slowed as I pulled onto my street, admiring each florally colored house with a small smile on my face. Gliding down the driveway, I leaned my bike against the garage and walked back towards the mailbox. I opened it and found our usual big pile of letters and junk mail.

Near the bottom though, there was a packet. It had my name on it in big bold letters. It was from Appalachian State University. I tore it open in my driveway, pulling a small piece of paper out of the front. Dylan Anderson, Congratulations. Congratulations.

You've been accepted...

I felt a funny little feeling rise in my chest, distant and familiar. A feeling of happiness and contentment. I looked up at the sky and held the envelope close to my chest, feeling that funny little feeling and basking in the cool afternoon air.

The sound of someone coming up behind me made me turn on my heel. Ida. She grinned at me, her eyes glinting happily with pride through her thick red glasses.

"I knew you could do it, kid."